Twenty-Five Gh

(Editor: W. Bob Holland)

Alpha Editions

This edition published in 2024

ISBN : 9789362519771

Design and Setting By
Alpha Editions
www.alphaedis.com
Email - info@alphaedis.com

As per information held with us this book is in Public Domain.
This book is a reproduction of an important historical work. Alpha Editions uses the best technology to reproduce historical work in the same manner it was first published to preserve its original nature. Any marks or number seen are left intentionally to preserve its true form.

Contents

PREFACE .... - 1 -
THE BLACK CAT. BY EDGAR ALLAN POE. .... - 2 -
THE FLAYED HAND. BY GUY DE MAUPASSANT. .... - 12 -
THE VENGEANCE OF A TREE.
 BY ELEANOR F. LEWIS. .... - 17 -
THE PARLOR-CAR GHOST. .... - 21 -
GHOST OF BUCKSTOWN INN. BY ARNOLD M.
ANDERSON. .... - 25 -
THE BURGLAR'S GHOST. .... - 29 -
A PHANTOM TOE. .... - 38 -
MRS. DAVENPORT'S GHOST. BY FREDERICK P.
SCHRADER. .... - 41 -
THE PHANTOM WOMAN. .... - 46 -
THE PHANTOM HAG. .... - 52 -
FROM THE TOMB. TRANSLATED FROM THE FRENCH OF
DE MAUPASSANT BY E. C. WAGGENER. .... - 55 -
SANDY'S GHOST. .... - 60 -
THE GHOSTS OF RED CREEK. BY S. T. .... - 65 -
THE SPECTRE BRIDE. .... - 68 -
HOW HE CAUGHT THE GHOST. .... - 71 -
GRAND-DAME'S GHOST STORY. BY C. D. .... - 77 -
A FIGHT WITH A GHOST. BY Q. E. D. .... - 81 -
COLONEL HALIFAX'S GHOST STORY. .... - 89 -
THE GHOST OF THE COUNT. .... - 100 -
THE OLD MANSION. .... - 106 -
A MISFIT GHOST. .... - 110 -
AN UNBIDDEN GUEST. .... - 113 -

THE DEAD WOMAN'S PHOTOGRAPH. ....- 116 -
THE GHOST OF A LIVE MAN. ....- 120 -
THE GHOST OF WASHINGTON. ....- 124 -

PREFACE

THIS collection of ghost stories owes its publication to an interest that I have long felt in the supernatural and in works of the imagination. As a child I was deeply concerned in tales of spooks, haunted houses, wraiths and specters and stories of weird experiences, clanking chains, ghostly sights and gruesome sounds always held me spellbound and breathless.

Experiences in editorial offices taught me that I was not alone in liking stories of mystery. The desire to know something of that existence that is veiled by Death is equally potent in old age and in youth, and men, women and children like to be thrilled and to have a "creepy" feeling along the spinal column as the result of reading of a visitor from beyond the grave.

This volume contains the most famous of the weird stories of Edgar Allan Poe, that master of this form of literature. "The Black Cat" contains all the needed element of mystery and supernatural, and yet the feline acts in a natural manner all of the time, and the story is quite possibly true. It is only in the manner of its telling that the tale becomes one that fittingly finds its place in this collection.

Guy de Maupassant, the clever Frenchman, is also represented by two effective bits of work, and other less widely known writers have also contributed stories that are worth reading, and when once read will be remembered. There is not a story among the twenty-five that is not worthy of close reading.

There has recently been a revival in interest in ghost stories. Many of the high-class magazines have within a few months printed stories with supernatural incidents, and writers whose names are known to all who read have turned their attention to this form of literature.

Whether or not the reader believe in ghosts, he cannot fail to be interested in this little book. Without venturing to express a positive opinion either way, I will only say with Hamlet: "There are more things in heaven and earth, Horatio, than are dreamt of in your philosophy."

W. BOB HOLLAND.

THE BLACK CAT.

BY EDGAR ALLAN POE.

FOR the most wild, yet most homely narrative which I am about to pen, I neither expect nor solicit belief. Mad indeed would I be to expect it, in a case where my very senses reject their own evidence. Yet, mad am I not—and very surely do I not dream. But to-morrow I die, and to-day I would unburden my soul. My immediate purpose is to place before the world, plainly, succinctly and without comment a series of mere household events. In their consequences, these events have terrified—have tortured—have destroyed me. Yet I will not attempt to expound them. To me they have presented little but horror, to many they will seem less terrible than baroques. Hereafter, perhaps, some intellect may be found which will reduce my phantasm to the commonplace—some intellect more calm, more logical, and far less excitable than my own, which will perceive in the circumstances I detail with awe nothing more than an ordinary succession of very natural causes and effects.

From my infancy I was noted for the docility and humanity of my disposition. My tenderness of heart was even so conspicuous as to make me the jest of my companions. I was especially fond of animals, and was indulged by my parents with a great variety of pets. With these I spent most of my time, and never was so happy as when feeding and caressing them. This peculiarity of character grew with my growth, and in my manhood I derived from it one of my principal sources of pleasure. To those who have cherished an affection for a faithful and sagacious dog, I need hardly be at the trouble of explaining the nature or the intensity of the gratification thus derivable. There is something in the unselfish and self-sacrificing love of a brute, which goes directly to the heart of him who has had frequent occasion to test the paltry friendship and gossamer fidelity of mere Man.

I married early, and was happy to find in my wife a disposition not uncongenial with my own. Observing my partiality for domestic pets she lost no opportunity of procuring those of the most agreeable kind. We had birds, goldfish, a fine dog, rabbits, a small monkey and a cat.

This latter was a remarkably large and beautiful animal, entirely black, and sagacious to an astonishing degree. In speaking of his intelligence, my wife, who at heart was not a little tinctured with superstition, made frequent allusion to the ancient popular notion, which regarded all black cats as witches in disguise. Not that she was ever serious upon this point—and I mention the matter at all for no better reason than that it happens, just now, to be remembered.

Pluto—this was the cat's name—was my favorite pet and playmate. I alone fed him, and he attended me wherever I went about the house. It was even with difficulty that I could prevent him from following me through the streets.

Our friendship lasted, in this manner, for several years, during which my general temperament and character—through the instrumentality of the fiend Intemperance—had (I blush to confess it) experienced a radical alteration for the worse. I grew, day by day, more moody, more irritable, more regardless of the feelings of others. I suffered myself to use intemperate language to my wife. At length I even offered her personal violence. My pets, of course, were made to feel the change in my disposition. I not only neglected them, but ill-used them. For Pluto, however, I still retained sufficient regard to restrain me from maltreating him, as I made no scruple of maltreating the rabbits, the monkey or even the dog, when by accident or through affection they came in my way. But my disease grew upon me—for what disease is like alcohol! And at length even Pluto, who was now becoming old, and consequently somewhat peevish—even Pluto began to experience the effects of my ill-temper.

One night, returning home much intoxicated from one of my haunts about town, I fancied that the cat avoided my presence. I seized him, when, in his fright at my violence, he inflicted a slight wound upon my hand with his teeth. The fury of a demon instantly possessed me. I knew myself no longer. My original soul seemed, at once, to take its flight from my body; and a more than fiendish malevolence, gin-nurtured, thrilled every fiber of my frame. I took from my waistcoat pocket a penknife, opened it, grasped the poor beast by the throat, and deliberately cut one of its eyes from the socket! I blush, I burn, I shudder while I pen the damnable atrocity.

When reason returned with the morning—when I had slept off the fumes of the night's debauch—I experienced a sentiment half of horror, half of remorse, for the crime of which I had been guilty; but it was, at best, a feeble and equivocal feeling, and the soul remained untouched. I again plunged into excess, and soon drowned in wine all memory of the deed.

In the meantime the cat slowly recovered.

"One night, returning home much intoxicated."

The socket of the lost eye presented, it is true, a frightful appearance, but he no longer appeared to suffer any pain. He went about the house as usual, but, as might be expected, fled in extreme terror at my approach. I had so much of my old heart left as to be at first grieved by this evident dislike on the part of a creature which had once so loved me. But this feeling soon gave place to irritation. And then came, as if to my final and irrevocable overthrow, the spirit of perverseness. Of this spirit philosophy takes no account. Yet I am not more sure that my soul lives than I am that perverseness is one of the primitive impulses of the human heart—one of the indivisible primary faculties or sentiments which give direction to the character of man. Who has not, hundreds of times, found himself committing a vile or silly action, for no other reason than because he knows he should not? Have we not a perpetual inclination, in the teeth of our best judgment, to violate that which is Law, merely because we understand it to be such? This spirit of perverseness, I say, came to my final overthrow. It was this unfathomable longing of the soul to vex itself—to offer violence to its own nature—to do wrong for the wrong's sake only—that urged me to continue and finally to consummate the injury I had inflicted upon the unoffending brute. One morning, in cold blood, I slipped a noose about its neck, and hung it to the limb of a tree; hung it with the tears streaming from my eyes and the bitterest remorse at my heart; hung it because I knew that it had loved me, and because I felt it had given me no offense; hung it because I knew that in so doing I was committing a sin—a deadly sin that would so jeopardize my immortal soul as to place it, if such a thing were possible—even beyond the reach of the infinite mercy of the most merciful and most terrible God.

On the night of the day on which this cruel deed was done, I was aroused from sleep by the cry of "fire!" The curtains of my bed were in flames. The whole house was blazing. It was with great difficulty that my wife, a servant and myself made our escape from the conflagration. The destruction was complete. My entire worldly wealth was swallowed up, and I resigned myself thenceforward to despair.

I am above the weakness of seeking to establish a sequence of cause and effect between the disaster and the atrocity. But I am detailing a chain of facts, and wish not to leave even a possible link imperfect. On the day succeeding the fire I visited the ruins. The walls, with one exception, had fallen in. This exception was found in a compartment wall, not very thick, which stood about the middle of the house, and against which had rested the head of my bed. The plastering had here, in great measure, resisted the action of the fire—a fact which I attributed to its having been recently spread. About this wall a dense crowd were collected, and many persons seemed to be examining a particular portion of it with very minute and eager attention. The words "strange!" "singular!" and other similar expressions excited my curiosity. I approached and saw, as if graven in bas-relief upon the white surface, the figure of a gigantic cat. The impression was given with an accuracy truly marvelous. There was a rope about the animal's neck.

When I first beheld this apparition—for I could scarcely regard it as less—my wonder and my terror were extreme. But at length reflection came to my aid. The cat, I remembered, had been hung in a garden adjacent to the house. Upon the alarm of fire this garden had been immediately filled by the crowd—by some one of whom the animal must have been cut from the tree and thrown through an open window into my chamber. This had probably been done with the view of arousing me from sleep. The falling of other walls had compressed the victim of my cruelty into the substance of the freshly spread plaster, the lime of which with the flames, and the ammonia from the carcass, had then accomplished the portraiture as I saw it.

Although I thus readily accounted to my reason, if not altogether to my conscience, for the

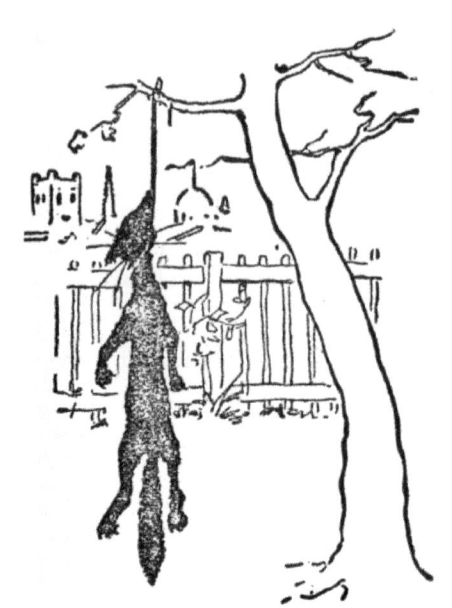

"Because I knew that it had loved me."

startling fact just detailed, it did not the less fail to make a deep impression upon my fancy. For months I could not rid myself of the phantasm of the cat; and, during this period, there came back into my spirit a half sentiment that seemed, but was not, remorse. I went so far as to regret the loss of the animal, and to look about me, among the vile haunts which I now habitually frequented, for another pet of the same species and of somewhat similar appearance, with which to supply its place.

One night as I sat, half stupefied, in a den of more than infamy, my attention was suddenly drawn to some black object, reposing upon the head of one of the immense hogsheads of gin, or of rum, which constituted the chief furniture of the apartment. I had been looking steadily at the top of this hogshead for some minutes, and what now caused me surprise was the fact that I had not sooner perceived the object thereupon. I approached it and touched it with my hand. It was a black cat—a very large one—fully as large as Pluto, and closely resembling him in every respect, but only Pluto had not a white hair upon any portion of his body; but this cat had a large, although indefinite, splotch of white, covering nearly the whole region of the breast.

Upon my touching him he immediately arose, purred loudly, rubbed against my hand, and appeared delighted with my notice. This, then, was the very creature of which I was in search. I at once offered to purchase it of the landlord; but this person made no claim to it—knew nothing of it—had never seen it before.

I continued my caresses, and when I prepared to go home the animal evinced a disposition to accompany me. I permitted it to do so, occasionally stooping and patting it as I proceeded. When it reached the house it domesticated itself at once, and became immediately a great favorite with my wife.

For my own part, I soon found a dislike to it arising within me. This was just the reverse of what I had anticipated; but—I know not how or why it was—its evident fondness for myself rather disgusted and annoyed me. By slow degrees these feelings of disgust and annoyance rose into the bitterness of hatred. I avoided the creature; a certain sense of shame, and the remembrance of my former deed of cruelty, preventing me from physically abusing it. I did not, for some weeks, strike, or otherwise violently ill use it; but gradually—very gradually—I came to look upon it with unutterable loathing, and to flee silently from its odious presence, as from the breath of a pestilence.

What added, no doubt, to my hatred of the beast, was the discovery, on the morning after I brought it home, that, like Pluto, it also had been deprived of one of its eyes. This circumstance, however, only endeared it to my wife, who, as I have already said, possessed, in a high degree, that humanity of feeling which had once been my distinguishing trait, and the source of many of my simplest and purest pleasures.

With my aversion to this cat, however, its partiality for myself seemed to increase. It followed my footsteps with a pertinacity which it would be difficult to make the reader comprehend. Whenever I sat it would crouch beneath my chair or spring upon my knees, covering me with its loathsome caresses. If I arose to walk it would get between my feet, and thus nearly throw me down, or, fastening its long and sharp claws in my dress, clamber, in this manner, to my breast. At such times, although I longed to destroy it with a blow, I was yet withheld from so doing, partly by a memory of my former crime, but chiefly—let me confess it at once—by absolute dread of the beast.

This dread was not exactly a dread of physical evil—and yet I should be at a loss how otherwise to define it. I am almost ashamed to own—yes, even in this felon's cell, I am almost ashamed to own—that the terror and horror with which the animal inspired me had been heightened by one of the merest chimeras it would be possible to conceive. My wife had called my attention more than once, to the character of the mark of white hair, of which I have spoken, and which

"The figure of a gigantic cat."

constituted the sole visible difference between the strange beast and the one I had destroyed. The reader will remember that this mark, although large, had been originally very indefinite; but, by slow degrees—degrees nearly imperceptible, and which for a long time my reason struggled to reject as fanciful—it had, at length, assumed a rigorous distinctness of outline. It was now the representation of an object that I shudder to name—and for this, above all, I loathed and dreaded, and would have rid myself of the monster had I dared—it was now I say the image of a hideous, of a ghastly thing—of the gallows! Oh, mournful and terrible engine of horror and of crime—of agony and of death!

And now was I indeed wretched beyond the wretchedness of mere humanity. And a brute beast, whose fellow I had contemptuously destroyed—a brute beast to work out for me—for me, a man, fashioned in the image of the High God—so much of insufferable woe. Alas! neither by day nor night knew I the blessing of rest any more. During the former the creature left me no moment alone, and in the latter I started hourly from dreams of unutterable fear, to find the hot breath of the thing upon my face, and its vast weight—an incarnate nightmare that I had no power to shake off—incumbent eternally upon my heart.

Beneath the pressure of torments such as these the feeble remnants of the good within me succumbed. Evil thoughts became my sole intimates—the darkest and most evil of thoughts. The moodiness of my usual temper increased to hatred of all things and of all mankind; while, from the sudden, frequent and ungovernable outbursts of a fury to which I now blindly abandoned myself, my uncomplaining wife, alas! was the most usual and the most patient of sufferers.

One day she accompanied me upon some household errand into the cellar of the old building, which our poverty compelled us to inhabit. The cat followed me down the steep stairs, and, nearly throwing me headlong, exasperated me to madness. Uplifting an axe, and forgetting, in my wrath, the childish dread which had hitherto stayed my hand, I aimed a blow at the animal which, of course, would have proved instantly fatal had it descended as I wished. But this blow was arrested by the hand of my wife. Goaded, by the interference, into a rage more than demoniacal, I withdrew my arm from her grasp, and buried the ax in her brain. She fell dead upon the spot, without a groan.

This hideous murder accomplished, I set myself forthwith, and with entire deliberation, to the task of concealing the body. I knew that I could not remove it from the house, either by day or by night, without the risk of being observed by the neighbors. Many projects entered my mind. At one period I thought of cutting the corpse into minute fragments and destroying them by fire. At another I resolved to dig a grave for it in the floor of the cellar. Again, I deliberated about casting it into the well in the yard—about packing it in a box, as if merchandise, with the usual arrangements, and so getting a porter to take it from the house. Finally I hit upon what I considered a far better expedient than either of these. I determined to wall it up in the cellar—as the monks of the middle ages are recorded to have walled up their victims.

For a purpose such as this the cellar was well adapted. Its walls were loosely constructed, and had lately been plastered throughout with a rough plaster, which the dampness of the atmosphere had prevented from hardening. Moreover, in one of the walls was a projection, caused by a false chimney, or fireplace, that had been filled up, and made to resemble the rest of the cellar. I made no doubt that I could readily displace the bricks at this point, insert the corpse, and wall the whole up as before, so that no eye could detect anything suspicious.

And in this calculation I was not deceived. By means of a crowbar I easily dislodged the bricks, and, having carefully deposited the body against the inner wall, I propped it in that position, while, with little trouble, I relaid the whole structure as it originally stood. Having

"An extraordinary cat."

procured mortar, sand and hair with every possible precaution, I prepared a plaster which could not be distinguished from the old, and with this I very carefully went over the new brickwork. When I had finished I felt satisfied that all was right. The wall did not present the slightest appearance of having been disturbed. The rubbish on the floor was picked up with the minutest care. I looked around triumphantly and said to myself, "Here, at least, then, my labor has not been in vain."

My next step was to look for the beast which had been the cause of so much wretchedness, for I had at length firmly resolved to put it to death. Had I been able to meet with it at the moment there could have been no doubt of its fate; but it appeared that the crafty animal had been alarmed at the violence of my previous anger and forebore to present itself in my present mood. It is impossible to describe or to imagine the deep, the blissful sense of relief which the absence of the detested creature occasioned in my bosom. It did not make its appearance during the night—and thus, for one night at least since its introduction into the house, I soundly and tranquilly slept—aye, slept, even with the burden of murder upon my soul!

The second and the third day passed, and still my tormentor came not. Once again I breathed as a free man. The monster, in terror, had fled the premises forever! I should behold it no more! My happiness was supreme! The guilt of my dark deed disturbed me but little. Some few inquiries had been made, but these had been readily answered. Even a search had been instituted—but, of course, nothing was to be discovered. I looked upon my future felicity as secured.

Upon the fourth day of the assassination a party of the police came very unexpectedly into the house and proceeded again to make a rigorous investigation of the premises. Secure, however, in the inscrutability of my place of concealment, I felt no embarrassment whatever. The officers bade me accompany them in their search. They left no nook or corner unexplored. At length, for the third or fourth time, they descended into the cellar. I quivered not in a muscle. My heart beat as calmly as that of one who slumbers in innocence. I walked the cellar from end to end. I folded my arms upon my bosom and roamed easily to and fro. The police were thoroughly satisfied and prepared to depart. The glee at my heart was too strong to be restrained. I burned to say but one word, by way of triumph, and to render doubly sure their assurance of my guiltlessness.

"Gentlemen," I said at last, as the party ascended the steps, "I delight to have allayed your suspicions. I wish you all health and a little more courtesy. By the by, gentlemen, this—this is a very well constructed house." (In the rabid desire to say something easily I scarcely knew what I uttered at all.) "I may say an excellently well constructed house. These walls—are you going, gentlemen?—these walls are solidly put together;" and here, through the mere frenzy of bravado, I rapped heavily, with a cane which I held in my hand, upon that very portion of the brickwork behind which stood the corpse of the wife of my bosom.

But may God shield and deliver me from the fangs of the Arch Fiend! No sooner had the reverberation of my blows sunk into silence than I was answered by a voice from within the tomb!—by a cry, at first muffled and broken, like the sobbing of a child, and then quickly swelling into one long, loud and continuous scream, utterly anomalous and inhuman—a howl!—a wailing shriek, half of horror and half of triumph, such as might have arisen only out of hell, conjointly from the throats of the damned in their agony and of the demons that exult in the damnation.

Of my own thoughts it is folly to speak. Swooning, I staggered to the opposite wall. For an instant the party upon the stairs remained motionless, through extremity of terror and of awe. In the next a dozen stout arms were toiling at the wall. It fell bodily. The corpse, already getting decayed and clotted with gore, stood erect before the eyes of the spectators. Upon its head, with red, extended mouth and solitary eye of fire, sat the hideous beast whose craft had seduced me into murder, and whose informing voice had consigned me to the hangman. I had walled the monster up within the tomb!

THE FLAYED HAND.

BY GUY DE MAUPASSANT.

ONE evening about eight months ago I met with some college comrades at the lodgings of our friend Louis R. We drank punch and smoked, talked of literature and art, and made jokes like any other company of young men. Suddenly the door flew open, and one who had been my friend since boyhood burst in like a hurricane.

"Guess where I come from?" he cried.

"I bet on the Mabille," responded one. "No," said another, "you are too gay; you come from borrowing money, from burying a rich uncle, or from pawning your watch." "You are getting sober," cried a third, "and, as you scented the punch in Louis' room, you came up here to get drunk again."

"You are all wrong," he replied. "I come from P., in Normandy, where I have spent eight days, and whence I have brought one of my friends, a great criminal, whom I ask permission to present to you."

With these words he drew from his pocket a long, black hand, from which the skin had been stripped. It had been severed at the wrist. Its dry and shriveled shape, and the narrow, yellowed nails still clinging to the fingers, made it frightful to look upon. The muscles, which showed that its first owner had been possessed of great strength, were bound in place by a strip of parchment-like skin.

"Just fancy," said my friend, "the other day they sold the effects of an old sorcerer, recently deceased, well known in all the country. Every Saturday night he used to go to witch gatherings on a broomstick; he practised the white magic and the black, gave blue milk to the cows, and made them wear tails like that of the companion of Saint Anthony. The old scoundrel always had a deep affection for this hand, which, he said, was that of a celebrated criminal, executed in 1736 for having thrown his lawful wife head first into a well—for which I do not blame him—and then hanging in the belfry the priest who had married him. After this double exploit he went away, and, during his subsequent career, which was brief but exciting, he robbed twelve travelers, smoked a score of monks in their monastery, and made a seraglio of a convent."

"But what are you going to do with this horror?" we cried.

"Eh! parbleu! I will make it the handle to my door-bell and frighten my creditors."

"My friend," said Henry Smith, a big, phlegmatic Englishman, "I believe that this hand is only a kind of Indian meat, preserved by a new process; I advise you to make bouillon of it."

"Rail not, messieurs," said, with the utmost sang froid, a medical student who was three-quarters drunk, "but if you follow my advice, Pierre, you will give this piece of human debris Christian burial, for fear lest its owner should come to demand it. Then, too, this hand has acquired some bad habits, for you know the proverb, 'Who has killed will kill.'"

"And who has drank will drink," replied the host as he poured out a big glass of punch for the student, who emptied it at a draught and slid dead drunk under the table. His sudden dropping out of the company was greeted with a burst of laughter, and Pierre, raising his glass and saluting the hand, cried:

"I drink to the next visit of thy master."

Then the conversation turned upon other subjects, and shortly afterward each returned to his lodgings.

*   *   *   *   *

About two o'clock the next day, as I was passing Pierre's door, I entered and found him reading and smoking.

"Well, how goes it?" said I. "Very well," he responded. "And your hand?" "My hand? Did you not see it on the bell-pull? I put it there when I returned home last night. But, apropos of this, what do you think? Some idiot, doubtless to play a stupid joke on me, came ringing at my door towards midnight. I demanded who was there, but as no one replied, I went back to bed again, and to sleep."

At this moment the door opened and the landlord, a fat and extremely impertinent person, entered without saluting us.

"Sir," said he, "I pray you to take away immediately that carrion which you have hung to your bell-pull. Unless you do this I shall be compelled to ask you to leave."

"Sir," responded Pierre, with much gravity, "you insult a hand which does not merit it. Know you that it belonged to a man of high breeding?"

The landlord turned on his heel and made his exit, without speaking. Pierre followed him, detached the hand and affixed it to the bell-cord hanging in his alcove.

"That is better," he said. "This hand, like the 'Brother, all must die,' of the Trappists, will give my thoughts a serious turn every night before I sleep."

At the end of an hour I left him and returned to my own apartment.

I slept badly the following night, was nervous and agitated, and several times awoke with a start. Once I imagined, even, that a man had broken into my room, and I sprang up and searched the closets and under the bed. Towards six o'clock in the morning I was commencing to doze at last, when a loud knocking at my door made me jump from my couch. It was my friend Pierre's servant, half dressed, pale and trembling.

"Ah, sir!" cried he, sobbing, "my poor master. Someone has murdered him."

I dressed myself hastily and ran to Pierre's lodgings. The house was full of people disputing together, and everything was in a commotion. Everyone was talking at the same time, recounting and commenting on the occurrence in all sorts of ways. With great difficulty I reached the bedroom, made myself known to those guarding the door and was permitted to enter. Four agents of police were standing in the middle of the apartment, pencils in hand, examining every detail, conferring in low voices and writing from time to time in their note-books. Two doctors were in consultation by the bed on which lay the unconscious form of Pierre. He was not dead, but his face was fixed in an expression of the most awful terror. His eyes were open their widest, and the dilated pupils seemed to regard fixedly, with unspeakable horror, something unknown and frightful. His hands were clinched. I raised the quilt, which covered his body from the chin downward, and saw on his neck, deeply sunk in the flesh, the marks of fingers. Some drops of blood spotted his shirt. At that moment one thing struck me. I chanced to notice that the shriveled hand was no longer attached to the bell-cord. The doctors had doubtless removed it to avoid the comments of those entering the chamber where the wounded man lay, because the appearance of this hand was indeed frightful. I did not inquire what had become of it.

I now clip from a newspaper of the next day the story of the crime with all the details that the police were able to procure:

"A frightful attempt was made yesterday on the life of young M. Pierre B., student, who belongs to one of the best families in Normandy. He returned home about ten o'clock in the evening, and excused his valet, Bouvin, from further attendance upon him, saying that he felt fatigued and was going to bed. Towards midnight Bouvin was suddenly awakened by the furious ringing of his master's bell. He was afraid, and lighted a lamp and waited. The bell was silent about a minute, then rang again with such vehemence that the domestic, mad with fright, flew from his room to awaken the concierge, who ran to summon the police, and, at the end of about fifteen minutes, two policemen forced open the door. A horrible sight met their eyes. The furniture was overturned, giving evidence of a fearful struggle between the victim and his assailant. In the middle of the room, upon his back, his body rigid, with livid face and frightfully dilated eyes, lay, motionless, young Pierre

B., bearing upon his neck the deep imprints of five fingers. Dr. Bourdean was called immediately, and his report says that the aggressor must have been possessed of prodigious strength and have had an extraordinarily thin and sinewy hand, because the fingers left in the flesh of the victim five holes like those from a pistol ball, and had penetrated until they almost met. There is no clue to the motive of the crime or to its perpetrator. The police are making a thorough investigation."

The following appeared in the same newspaper next day:

"M. Pierre B., the victim of the frightful assault of which we published an account yesterday, has regained consciousness after two hours of the most assiduous care by Dr. Bourdean. His life is not in danger, but it is strongly feared that he has lost his reason. No trace has been found of his assailant."

My poor friend was indeed insane. For seven months I visited him daily at the hospital where we had placed him, but he did not recover the light of reason. In his delirium strange words escaped him, and, like all madmen, he had one fixed idea: he believed himself continually pursued by a specter. One day they came for me in haste, saying he was worse, and when I arrived I found him dying. For two hours he remained very calm, then, suddenly, rising from his bed in spite of our efforts, he cried, waving his arms as if a prey to the most awful terror: "Take it away! Take it away! It strangles me! Help! Help!" Twice he made the circuit of the room, uttering horrible screams, then fell face downward, dead.

* * * * *

As he was an orphan I was charged to take his body to the little village of P., in Normandy, where his parents were buried. It was the place from which he had arrived the evening he found us drinking punch in Louis R.'s room, when he had presented to us the flayed hand. His body was inclosed in a leaden coffin, and four days afterwards I walked sadly beside the old cure, who had given him his first lessons, to the little cemetery where they dug his grave. It was a beautiful day, and sunshine from a cloudless sky flooded the earth. Birds sang from the blackberry bushes where many a time when we were children we had stolen to eat the fruit. Again I saw Pierre and myself creeping along behind the hedge and slipping through the gap that we knew so well, down at the end of the little plot where they bury the poor. Again we would return to the house with cheeks and lips black with the juice of the berries we had eaten. I looked at the bushes; they were covered with fruit; mechanically I picked some and bore it to my mouth. The cure had opened his breviary, and was muttering his prayers in a low voice. I heard at the end of the walk the spades of the grave-diggers who were opening the tomb. Suddenly they called out, the cure closed his book, and we went to see what they wished of us. They had found a coffin; in digging a stroke of the pickaxe had started the cover, and we perceived within a skeleton of unusual stature, lying on its back, its hollow eyes seeming yet to menace and defy us. I was troubled, I know not why, and almost afraid.

"Hold!" cried one of the men, "look there! One of the rascal's hands has been severed at the wrist. Ah, here it is!" and he picked up from beside the body a huge withered hand, and held it out to us.

"See," cried the other, laughing, "see how he glares at you, as if he would spring at your throat to make you give him back his hand."

"Go," said the cure, "leave the dead in peace, and close the coffin. We will make poor Pierre's grave elsewhere."

The next day all was finished, and I returned to Paris, after having left fifty francs with the old cure for masses to be said for the repose of the soul of him whose sepulchre we had troubled.

THE VENGEANCE OF A TREE.

BY ELEANOR F. LEWIS.

THROUGH the windows of Jim Daly's saloon, in the little town of C——, the setting sun streamed in yellow patches, lighting up the glasses scattered on the tables and the faces of several men who were gathered near the bar. Farmers mostly they were, with a sprinkling of shopkeepers, while prominent among them was the village editor, and all were discussing a startling piece of news that had spread through the town and its surroundings. The tidings that Walter Stedman, a laborer on Albert Kelsey's ranch, had assaulted and murdered his employer's daughter, had reached them, and had spread universal horror among the people.

A farmer declared that he had seen the deed committed as he walked through a neighboring lane, and, having always been noted for his cowardice, instead of running to the girl's aid, had hailed a party of miners who were returning from their mid-day meal through a field near by. When they reached the spot, however, where Stedman (as they supposed) had done his black deed, only the girl lay there, in the stillness of death. Her murderer had taken the opportunity to fly. The party had searched the woods of the Kelsey estate, and just as they were nearing the house itself the appearance of Walter Stedman, walking in a strangely unsteady manner toward it, made them quicken their pace.

He was soon in custody, although he had protested his innocence of the crime. He said that he had just seen the body himself on his way to the station, and that when they had found him he was going to the house for help. But they had laughed at his story and had flung him into the tiny, stifling calaboose of the town.

What were their proofs? Walter Stedman, a young fellow of about twenty-six, had come from the city to their quiet town, just when times were at their hardest, in search of work. The most of the men living in the town were honest fellows, doing their work faithfully, when they could get it, and when they had socially asked Stedman to have a drink with them, he had refused in rather a scornful manner. "That infernal city chap," he was called, and their hate and envy increased in strength when Albert Kelsey had employed him in preference to any of themselves. As time went on, the story of Stedman's admiration for Margaret Kelsey had gone afloat, with the added information that his employer's daughter had repulsed him, saying that she would not marry a common laborer. So Stedman, when this news reached his employer's ears, was discharged, and this, then, was his revenge! For them, these proofs were sufficient to pronounce him guilty.

Yet that afternoon, as Stedman, crouched on the floor of the calaboose, grew hopeless in the knowledge that no one would believe his story, and that his undeserved punishment would be swift and sure, a tramp, boarding a freight car several miles from the town, sped away from the spot where his crime had been committed, and knew that forever its shadow would follow him.

From the tiny window of his prison Walter Stedman could see the red glow of the heavens that betokened the setting of the sun. So the red sun of his life was soon to set, a life that had been innocent of all crime, and that now was to be ended for a deed that he had never committed. Most prominent of all the visions that swept through his mind was that of Margaret Kelsey, lying as he had first found her, fresh from the hands of her murderer. But there was another of a more tender nature. How long he and Margaret had tried to keep their secret, until Walter could be promoted to a higher position, so that he could ask for her hand with no fear of the father's antagonism! Then came the remembrance of an afternoon meeting between the two in the woods of the Kelsey estate—how, just as they were parting, Walter had heard footsteps near them, and, glancing sharply around, saw an evil, scowling, murderous face peering through the brush. He had started toward it, but the owner of the countenance had taken himself hurriedly off.

The gossiping townspeople had misconstrued this romance, and when Albert Kelsey had heard of this clandestine meeting from the man who was later on to appear as a leader of the mob, and that he had discharged Stedman, they had believed that the young man had formally proposed and had been rejected. But justice had gone wrong, as it had done innumerable times before, and will again. An innocent man was to be hanged, even without the comfort of a trial, while the man who was guilty was free to wander where he would.

That autumn night the darkness came quickly, and only the stars did their best to light the scene. A body of men, all masked, and having as a leader one who had ever since Stedman's arrival in town, cherished a secret hatred of the young man, dragged Stedman from the calaboose and tramped through the town, defying all, defying even God himself. Along the highway, and into Farmer Brown's "cross cut," they went, vigilantly guarding their prisoner, who, with the lanterns lighting up his haggard face, walked among them with the lagging step of utter hopelessness.

"That's a good tree," their leader said, presently, stopping and pointing out a spreading oak; when the slipknot was adjusted and Stedman had stepped on the box, he added: "If you've got anything to say, you'd better say it now."

"I am innocent, I swear before God," the doomed man answered; "I never took the life of Margaret Kelsey."

"Give us your proof," jeered the leader, and when Stedman kept a despairing silence, he laughed shortly.

"Ready, men!" he gave the order. The box was kicked aside, and then—only a writhing body swung to and fro in the gloom.

In front of the men stood their leader, watching the contortions of the body with silent glee. "I'll tell you a secret, boys," he said suddenly. "I was after that poor murdered girl myself. A d—— little chance I had; but, by ——, he had just as little!"

A pause—then: "He's shunted this earth. Cut him down, you fellows!"

* * * * *

"It's no use, son. I'll give up the blasted thing as a bad job. There's something queer about that there tree. Do you see how its branches balance it? We have cut the trunk nearly in two, but it won't come down. There's plenty of others around; we'll take one of them. If I'd a long rope with me I'd get that tree down, and yet the way the thing stands it would be risking a fellow's life to climb it. It's got the devil in it, sure."

So old Farmer Brown shouldered his axe and made for another tree, his son following. They had sawed and chopped and chopped and sawed, and yet the tall white oak, with its branches jutting out almost as regularly as if done by the work of a machine, stood straight and firm.

Farmer Brown, well known for his weak, cowardly spirit, who in beholding the murder of Albert Kelsey's daughter, had in his fright mistaken the criminal, now in his superstition let the oak stand, because its well-balanced position saved it from falling, when other trees would have been down. And so this tree, the same one to which an innocent man had been hanged, was left—for other work.

It was a bleak, rainy night—such a night as can be found only in central California. The wind howled like a thousand demons, and lashed the trees together in wild embraces. Now and then the weird "hoot, hoot!" of an owl came softly from the distance in the lulls of the storm, while the barking of coyotes woke the echoes of the hills into sounds like fiendish laughter.

In the wind and rain a man fought his path through the bush and into Farmer Brown's "cross cut," as the shortest way home. Suddenly he stopped, trembling, as if held by some unseen impulse. Before him rose the white oak, wavering and swaying in the storm.

"Good God! it's the tree I swung Stedman from!" he cried, and a strange fear thrilled him.

His eyes were fixed on it, held by some undefinable fascination. Yes, there on one of the longest branches a small piece of rope still dangled. And then, to the murderer's excited vision, this rope seemed to lengthen, to form at the end into a slipknot, a knot that encircled a purple neck, while below it writhed and swayed the body of a man!

"Damn him!" he muttered, starting toward the hanging form, as if about to help the rope in its work of strangulation; "will he forever follow me? And yet he deserved it, the black-hearted villain! He took her life——"

He never finished the sentence. The white oak, towering above him in its strength, seemed to grow like a frenzied, living creature. There was a sudden splitting sound, then came a crash, and under the fallen tree lay Stedman's murderer, crushed and mangled.

From between the broken trunk and the stump that was left, a gray, dim shape sprang out, and sped past the man's still form, away into the wild blackness of the night.

THE PARLOR-CAR GHOST.

ALL draped with blue denim—the seaside cottage of my friend, Sara Pyne. She asked me to go there with her when she opened it to have it set in order for the summer. She confessed that she felt a trifle nervous at the idea of entering it alone. And I am always ready for an excursion. So much blue denim rather surprised me, because blue is not complimentary to Sara's complexion—she always wears some shade of red, by preference. She perceived my wonder; she is very near-sighted, and therefore sees everything by some sort of sixth sense.

"You do not like my portieres and curtains and table-covers," said she. "Neither do I. But I did it to accommodate. And now he rests well in his grave, I hope."

"Whose grave, for pity's sake?"

"Mr. J. Billington Price's."

"And who is he? He doesn't sound interesting."

"Then I will tell you about him," said Sara, taking a seat directly in front of one of those curtains. "Last autumn I was leaving this place for New York, traveling on the fast express train known as the Flying Yankee. Of course, I thought of the Flying Dutchman and Wagner's musical setting of the uncanny legend, and how different things are in these days of steam, etc. Then I looked out of the window at the landscape, the horizon that seemed to wheel in a great curve as the train sped on. Every now and then I had an impression at the 'tail of the eye' that a man was sitting in a chair three or four numbers in front of me on the opposite side of the car. Each time that I saw this shape I looked at the chair and ascertained that it was unoccupied. But it was an odd trick of vision. I raised my lorgnette, and the chair showed emptier than before. There was nobody in it, certainly. But the more I knew that it was vacant the more plainly I saw the man. Always with the corner of my eye. It made me nervous. When passengers entered the car I dreaded lest they might take that seat. What would happen if they should? A bag was put in the chair—that made me uncomfortable. The bag was removed at the next station. Then a baby was placed in the seat. It began to laugh as though someone had gently tickled it. There was something odd about that chair—thirteen was its number. When I looked away from it the impression was strong upon me that some person sitting there was watching me.

"Really, it would not do to humor such fancies. So I touched the electric button, asked the porter to bring me a table, and taking from my bag a pack of cards, proceeded to divert myself with a game of patience. I was puzzling where to put a seven of spades. 'Where can it go?' I murmured to myself. A voice behind me prompted: 'Play the four of diamonds on the five, and you can do it.' I started. The only occupants of the car, besides me, were a bridal couple, a mother with three little children, and a typical preacher of one of the straitest sects. Who had spoken? 'Play up the four, madam,' repeated this voice.

"I looked fearfully over my shoulder. At first I saw a bluish cloud, like cigar smoke, but inodorous. Then the vision cleared, and I saw a young man whom I knew by a subtle intuition to be the occupant, seen and not seen, of chair number thirteen. Evidently he was a traveling salesman—and a ghost. Of course, a drummer's ghost sounds ridiculous—they're so extremely alive! Or else you would expect a dead drummer to be particularly dead and not 'walk.' This was a most commonplace-looking ghost, cordial, pushing, businesslike. At the same time, his face had an expression of utter despair and horror which made him still more preposterous. Of course it is not nice to let a stranger speak to one, even on so impersonal a topic as a four of diamonds. But a ghost—there can't be any rule of etiquette about talking with a ghost! My dear, it was dreadful! That forward creature showed me how to play all the cards, and then begged me to lay them out again, in order that he might give me some clever points. I was too much amazed and disturbed to speak. I could only place the cards at his suggestion. This I did so as not to appear to be listening to the empty air, and be supposed to be a crazy woman. Presently the ghost spoke again, and told me his story.

"'Madam,' he said, 'I have been riding back and forth on this car ever since February 22, 189——. Seven months and eleven days. All this time I have not exchanged a word with anyone. For a drummer, that is pretty hard, you may believe! You know the story of the Flying Dutchman? Well, that is very nearly my case. A curse is upon me and will not be removed until some kind soul——. But I'm getting ahead of my text. That day there were four of us, traveling for different houses. One of the boys was in wool, one in baking powder, one in boots and shoes, and myself in cotton goods. We met on the road, took seats together and fell into talking shop.

"'Those fellows told big lies about their sales, Washington's Birthday though it was. The baking powder man raised the amount of the bills of goods which he had sold better than a whole can of his stuff could have done. I admitted the straight truth, that I had not yet been able to make a sale. And then I swore—not in a light-minded, chipper style of verbal trimmings, but a great, round, heaven-defying oath—that I would sell a case of blue denims on that trip if it took me forever. We became dry with talk, and when the train stopped at Rivermouth, we went out to have some beer. It is good there, you know—pardon me, I forgot that I was speaking to a lady. Well, we had to run to get aboard. I missed my footing, fell under the wheels, and the next thing that I knew they were holding an inquest over my remains; while I, disemboweled, was sitting on a corner of the undertaker's table, wondering which of the coroner's jury was likely to want a case of blue denims.

"'Then I remembered my wicked oath, and understood that I was a soul doomed to wander until I could succeed in selling that bill of goods. I spoke once or twice, offering the denims under value, but nobody noticed me. Verdict: accidental death; negligence of deceased; railroad corporation not to blame; deceased got out for beer at his own risk. The other drummers took charge of the remains, and wrote a beautiful letter to my relatives about my social qualities and my impressive conversation. I wish it had been less impressive that time! I might have lied about my sales, or I might have said that I hoped for better luck. But after that oath there was nothing for it. Back and forth, back and forth, on this road, in chair number thirteen, to all eternity. Nobody suspects my presence. They sit on my knees—I'm playing in luck when it is a nice baby as it was this afternoon! They pile wraps, bags, even railway literature on me. They play cards under my nose—and what duffers some of them are! You, madam, are the first person who has perceived me; and therefore I ventured to speak to you, meaning no offense. I can see that you are sorry for me. Now, if you recall the story of the Flying Dutchman, he was saved by the charity of a good woman. In fact, Senta married him. Now I'm not asking anything of that size. I see that you wear a wedding ring, and no doubt you make some man's happiness. I wasn't a marrying man myself, and, naturally, am not a marrying ghost. And that has nothing to do with the matter anyway. But if you could—I don't suppose you would have any use for them—but if you were disposed to do a turn of good, solid, Christian charity—I should be everlastingly grateful, and you may have that case of denims at $72.50. And that quality is quoted to-day at $80. Does it go, madam?'

"The speech of the poor ghost was not very eloquent, but his eyes had an intense, eager glare, which was terrible. Something—pity, fear, I do not know what—compelled me. I decided to do without that white and gold evening cloak. Instead, I gave $72.50 to the ghost and took from him a receipt for the sum, signed J. Billington Price. Then he smiled contentedly, thanked me with emotion, and returned to chair number thirteen. Several times on the journey, although I did not perceive him again, I felt dazed. When the train arrived at New York, and I, with the other passengers, dismounted, it seemed to me that a strong hand passed under my elbow, steadying me down the steps. As I walked the length of the station my bag—not heavy at any time—appeared to become weightless. I believe that the parlor-car ghost walked beside me, carrying the bag, whose handle still remained in my other hand. Indeed, once or twice I thought I felt the touch of cold fingers against mine. Since then I have no reason to suppose that the poor ghost is not at rest. I hope he is.

"But I never expected nor wished for the blue denims. The next day, however, a dray belonging to a great wholesale house backed up to our door and delivered a case of denims, with a receipted bill for the same. What was I to do? I could not go about selling blue denims; I could not give them away without exciting comment. So I furnished the cottage with them—and you know the effect on my complexion. Pity me, dear! And credit me, frivolous woman as I am, with having saved a soul at the expense of my own vanity. My story is told. What do you think about it?"

GHOST OF BUCKSTOWN INN.

BY ARNOLD M. ANDERSON.

SEVERAL travel-worn drummers sat in the lobby exchanging yarns. It was Rodney Green's turn, and he looked wise and began his tale.

"I don't claim, by any means, that the belief in ghosts is a general thing in Arkansas, but I do say that I had an experience out there a few years ago.

"It was late in the fall, and I happened to be in the village of Buckstown, which desecrates a very limited portion of the State. The town is about as small and dirty a place as ever I saw, and the Buckstown Inn is not much above the general character of the place. The region is inhabited by natives who still cling to all sorts of foolish superstitions. The inn, in the ante-bellum days, was kept by one who was said to be the meanest and most crabbed of mortals. The old demon was as miserly as he was mean, and all his narrow life he hoarded his filthy lucre with fiendish greed. Report had it also that he had even murdered his patrons in their beds for their money. What the facts actually were I don't know, but even to this day the old inn is held in suspicion. A lingering effect of former horrors still clouds its memory.

"The present proprietor, Bunk Watson—his real name is Bunker, I believe—is an altogether different sort of chap—a Southern type, in fact—one of those shiftless, heedless, happy-go-lucky mortals who loves strong whiskey and who chews an enormous quid of black tobacco and smokes a corncob pipe at the same time.

"When the former keeper 'shuffled off,' his property fell to a distant relative, the present keeper, who, with his family, immediately moved in from a neighboring hamlet and took possession. It was well known that the old proprietor had accumulated considerable wealth during his sojourn among the living, but all efforts to discover any treasure upon the premises had failed, and now the idea of ever finding it was practically given up. As far as Bunk was concerned, the matter troubled him little. He had a hard-working wife who ran things the best she could under the circumstances, and saw that his meals were forthcoming at their respective intervals. What more could he wish? Why should he care if there was a treasure buried upon his place? Indeed, it would have been a sore puzzle for him to know what to do with a fortune unless perhaps his wife came to his aid.

"Among the stories that hovered in the history of the Buckstown Inn was one which involved a ghost. In the room where the former keeper had died peculiar noises were heard at unearthly hours: sighing, moaning, and, in fact, all the other indications which point to the existence of ghosts, were said to be present. On account of this the chamber had long since been abandoned.

"I listened with keen interest to the wonderful tales about the haunted room, and then suddenly resolved to investigate—to sleep in that chamber that very night and see for myself all that was to be seen. I told Buck of my purpose. He shook his head, shrugged his shoulders, but instead of warning me and offering a flood of protests, as I expected, he merely took his pipe from his mouth, let fly a quart or so of yellowish juice from between a pair of brown-stained lips, and, opening one corner of his wide mouth, lazily called out: 'Jane.' His wife appeared, and he intimated that I should settle the matter with the 'old woman.' The prospect of a fee persuaded the wife, and off she went to arrange for my bed in that ill-fated room.

"At nine o'clock that evening I bid the family good-night, took my candle, ascended the rickety stairs and entered the chamber of horrors. The atmosphere was heavy and had a peculiar odor that was not at all pleasing. However, I latched the door and was soon in bed. Having propped myself up with pillows, I was prepared to await the coming of the ghost.

"Overhead the dusty rafters, which once had experienced the sensation of being whitewashed, but which were now a dirty, yellowish color, were hung with a fantastic array of cobwebs. The flickering light of the candle reflected upon the walls and against the ceiling a pyramid of grotesque shapes, and with this effect being continually disturbed by the swaying cobwebs, the whole caused the room to appear rather ghostly after all, and especially so to an imaginative mind.

"I waited and waited for hours, it seemed, but still no ghost. Perhaps it was afraid of my candle light, so I blew it out. No sooner had I done this and settled back in bed again than a white hand appeared through the door, then a whole figure—at last the ghost had come, a white and sheeted ghost!

"It had come right through the door, although it was locked, and now it advanced toward the bed. Raising its long, white arm, it pointed a bony finger at me, and then commanded: 'Come with me!' Thereupon it turned to the door, while instantly I jumped out of bed to follow. Some unseen power compelled me to obey. The door flew open and the ghost led me down the stairs, through long halls into the cellar, through mysterious underground corridors, upstairs again, in and out rooms which I never dreamed were to be found in that old rambling inn. Finally, through a small door in the rear, we left the house. I was in my sleeping garments, but no matter, I had to follow.

"The white form, with a slow and measured tread and as silent as death, led the way into the orchard. There, under a tree at the farther end, it pointed to the ground, and in the same ghostly tones before used, said:

"'Here you will find a great treasure buried.'

"The ghost then disappeared, and I saw it no more. I stood dazed and trembling. Upon recovering my wits I started to dig, but the chill of the night air and the scantiness of my night robes made such labor impracticable. So I decided to leave some mark to identify the place and come around again at daybreak. I reached up and broke off a limb. Overcome with my night's exertions I slept the next morning until a loud rapping on my door and a croaking voice warned me that it was noon.

"I had intended to leave Buckstown Inn that day, but, prompted by curiosity and anxious to investigate, I unpacked my gripsack for a comfortable stay.

"You must understand that this was my first experience with a ghost, and I feared I might never see another.

"At breakfast my landlady waited on me in silence, though once I detected her eyes following me with a peculiar expression. She wanted to ask me how I enjoyed the night, but I would not gratify her by volunteering a word.

"My host was more outspoken.

"'Reckon ye didn't get much sleep,' said he, with a queer smile.

"'Did you hear anything?' I asked.

"'Well, I did—ye-es,' he said, with a drawl. 'But ye didn't disturb me any. I knew ye'd hev trouble when ye went in thet room ter sleep.'

"That afternoon I slipped out to the tree. But to my amazement I found that the twig I had broken from the branches was gone. Finally I found under the lower trunk of an apple tree an open place from which a small branch had evidently been wrested. But on looking further, I discovered that every apple tree in the orchard had been similarly disfigured.

"'More mysterious than ever,' I said; 'but to-night shall decide.'

"That night I pleaded weariness, which no one seemed inclined to question, and sought my couch earlier.

"'Goin' ter try it again?' asked my host.

"'Yes; and I'll stay all winter but what I'll get even with that ghost,' I said.

"That night I kept the candle burning until midnight, when I blew it out.

"Instantly the room was flooded with a soft light, and at the foot of the bed stood my ghost, the identical ghost of last night.

"Again the bony finger beckoned and a sepulchral voice whispered, 'Follow me!' I sprang from the bed, but the figure darted ahead of me. It flew through the doorway and down the stairs, and I after it. At the foot of the staircase an unseen hand reached forward and caught my foot and I fell sprawling headlong.

"But in a second I was on my feet and pursuing the ghost. It had gained on me a few yards, but I was quicker, and just as we reached the outside door I nearly touched its robes. They sent a chill through my frame, and I nearly gave up the pursuit.

"As it passed through the doorway it turned and gave me one look, and I caught the same malignant light in its eyes that I remembered from the night before.

"In the open orchard I felt sure I could catch it.

"But my ghost had no intention of allowing me any such opportunity. To my disgust, it darted backward and into the house, slamming the door in my face.

"In my frenzy of fear and chagrin I threw myself against the oaken door with such force that its rusty old hinges yielded and I landed in the big front room of the inn just in time to see the white skirts of the ghost flit up the stairs.

"Upstairs I flew after it, and into an old chamber. There, huddled in a corner, I saw it. In the minute's delay it had secured a lighted candle and, as I entered, it advanced to daunt me with bony arm upraised to a great height.

"'Caught!' I cried, throwing my arms around the figure. And I had made the acquaintance of a real live ghost.

"The white robes fell, and I saw revealed my hostess of Buckstown Inn.

"Next morning, when I threatened to call the police, she confessed to me that she masqueraded as a ghost to draw visitors to the out-of-the-way old place, and that she found its tale of being haunted highly profitable to her."

THE BURGLAR'S GHOST.

I AM not an imaginative man, and no one who knows me can say that I have ever indulged in sentimental ideas upon any subject. I am rather predisposed, in fact, to look at everything from a purely practical standpoint, and this quality has been further developed in me by the fact that for twenty years I have been an active member of the detective police force at Westford, a large town in one of our most important manufacturing districts. A policeman, as most people will readily believe, has to deal with so much practical life that he has small opportunity for developing other than practical qualities, and he is more apt to believe in tangible things than in ideas of a somewhat superstitious nature. However, I was once under the firm conviction that I had been largely helped up the ladder of life by the ghost of a once well-known burglar. I have told the story to many, and have heard it commented upon in various fashions. Whether the comments were satirical or practical, it made no difference to me; I had a firm faith at that time in the truth of my tale.

Eighteen years ago I was a plain clothes officer at Westford. I was then twenty-three years of age, and very anxious about two matters. First and foremost I desired promotion; second, I wished to be married. Of course I was more eager about the second than the first, because my sweetheart, Alice Moore, was one of the prettiest and cleverest girls in the town; but I put promotion first for the simple reason that with me promotion must come before marriage. Knowing this, I was always on the lookout for a chance of distinguishing myself, and I paid such attention to my duties that my superiors began to notice me, and foretold a successful career for me in the future.

One evening in the last week of September, 1873, I was sitting in my lodgings wondering what I could do to earn the promotion which I so earnestly wished for. Things were quiet just then in Westford, and I am afraid I half wished that something dreadful might occur if I only could have a share in it. I was pursuing this train of thought when I suddenly heard a voice say, "Good evening, officer."

I turned sharply around. It was almost dusk and my lamp was not lighted. For all that, I could see clearly enough a man who was sitting by a chest of drawers that stood between the door and the window. His chair stood between the drawers and the door, and I concluded that he had quietly entered my room and seated himself before addressing me.

"Good evening!" I replied. "I didn't hear you come in."

He laughed when I said that—a low, chuckling, rather sly laugh. "No," he said, "I dessay not, officer. I'm a very quiet sort of person. You might say, in fact, noiseless. Just so."

I looked at him narrowly, feeling considerably surprised and astonished at his presence. He was a thickly built man, with a square face and heavy chin. His nose was small, but aggressive; his eyes were little and overshadowed by heavy eyebrows; I could see them twinkle when he spoke. As for his dress, it was in keeping with his face.

He wore a rough suit of woolen or frieze; a thick, gayly colored Belcher neckerchief encircled his bull-like throat, and in his big hands he continually twirled and twisted a fur cap, made apparently out of the skin of some favorite dog. As he sat there smiling at me and saying nothing, it made me feel uncomfortable.

"What do you want with me?" I asked.

"Just a little matter o' business," he answered.

"You should have gone to the office," I said. "We're not supposed to do business at home."

"Right you are, guv'nor," he replied; "but I wanted to see you. It's you that's got to do my job. If I'd ha' seen the superintendent he might ha' put somebody else on to it. That wouldn't ha' suited me. You see, officer, you're young, and nat'rally eager-like for promotion. Eh?"

"What is it you want?" I inquired again.

"Ain't you eager to be promoted?" he reiterated. "Ain't you now, officer?"

I saw no reason why I should conceal the fact, even from this strange visitor. I admitted that I was eager for promotion.

"Ah!" he said, with a satisfied smile; "I'm glad o' that. It'll make you all the keener. Now, officer, you listen to me. I'm a-goin' to put you on to a nice little job. Ah! I dessay you'll be a sergeant before long, you will. You'll be complimented and praised for your clever conduck in this 'ere affair. Mark my words if you ain't."

"Out with it," I said, fancying I saw through the man's meaning. "You're going to split on some of your pals, I suppose, and you'll want a reward."

He shook his head. "A reward," he said, "wouldn't be no use to me at all—no, not if it was a thousand pounds. No, it ain't nothing to do with reward. But now, officer, did you ever hear of Light Toed Jim?"

Light Toed Jim! I should have been a poor detective if I had not. Why, the man known under that sobriquet was one of the cleverest burglars and thieves in England, and had enjoyed such a famous career that his name was a household word. At that moment there was an additional interest attached to him. He had been convicted of burglary at the Northminster assizes in 1871, and sentenced to ten years' penal servitude. After serving nearly two years of his time he had escaped from Portland, getting away in such clever fashion that he had never been heard of since. Where he was no one could say; but lately there had been a strong suspicion among the police that Light Toed Jim was at his old tricks again.

"Light Toed Jim!" I repeated. "I should think so. Why, what do you know about him?"

He smiled and nodded his head. "Light Toed Jim," said he, "is in Westford at this 'ere hidentical moment. Listen to me, officer. Light Toed Jim is a-goin' to crack a crib to-night. Said crib is the mansion of Miss Singleton, that 'ere rich old lady as lives out on the Mapleton Road. You know her—awfully rich, with naught but women servants and animals about the place. There's some very valyable plate there. That's what Light Toed Jim's after. He'll get in through the scullery window about 1 a. m., then he'll pass through the back and front kitchens and into the butler's pantry—only it's a butleress, 'cos there ain't no men at all—and there he'll set to work on the safe. Some of his late pals in Portland give him the tip about this 'ere job."

"How did you come to hear of it?" I asked.

"Never mind, guv'nor. You wouldn't understand. Now, I wants you to be up there to-night and to nab Light Toed Jim red-handed, so to speak. It'll mean promotion for you, and it'll suit me down to the ground. You wants to be about and to watch him enter. Then follow him and dog him. And be armed, officer, for Jim'll fight like a tiger if you don't draw his teeth first."

"Now, look here, my man," said I, "this is all very well, but it's all irregular. You must just tell me who you are and how you come to be in Light Toed Jim's secrets, and I'll put it down in black and white."

I turned away from him to get my writing materials. I was not half a minute with my back to him, but when I turned round he was gone. The door was shut, but I had heard no sound from it either opening or shutting. Quick as thought I darted to it, tore it wide open, and looked down the narrow staircase. There was no one there. I ran hastily downstairs into the passage, and found my landlady, Mrs. Marriner, standing at the open door with a female friend. "Mrs. Marriner," I said, breaking in upon their conversation, "which way did that man go who came downstairs just now?"

Mrs. Marriner looked at me strangely. "There ain't been no man come downstairs, Mr. Parker," said she; "leastways, not this good three-quarters of an hour, which me and Missis Higgins 'ere, as 'ave come out to take an airing, her having been ironin' all this blessed day, has been standin' 'ere all the time and ain't never seen a soul."

"Nonsense," I said. "A man came down from my room just now—the man you sent up twenty minutes since."

Mrs. Marriner looked at me with an expression betokening the most profound astonishment. Mrs. Higgins sighed deeply.

"Mr. Parker," said Mrs. Marriner, "sorry am I to say it, sir, but you're either intoxicated or else you're a-sickening for brain fever, sir. There ain't no person entered this door, in or out, for nigh onto an hour, as me and Missis Higgins 'ere will take our Bible oaths on."

I went upstairs and looked in the rooms on either side of mine. The man was not there. I looked under my bed, and of course he was not there. He must have gone downstairs. But then the women must have seen him. There was only one door to the house. I gave it up in despair and began to smoke my pipe. By the time I had drawn the last whiff I decided that if anyone was "intoxicated," it was probably Mrs. Marriner and Mrs. Higgins, and that my strange visitor had departed by the door. I was not going to believe that he had anything supernatural about him.

I had no duty that night, and as the hours wore on I found myself stern in my resolve to go up to Miss Singleton's house and see what I could make out of my informant's story. It was my opinion that my late visitor was a whilom "pal" of Light Toed Jim, and that having become aware of the latter's plot, he had, for some reason of his own, decided to split on his old chum. Thieves' disagreement is an honest man's opportunity, and I determined to solve the truth of the story told me. Lest it should come to nothing, I decided not to report the matter to my chief. If I could really capture Light Toed Jim, my success would be all the more brilliant by being suddenly sprung upon the authorities.

I made my plan of action rapidly. I took a revolver with me and went up to Miss Singleton's house. Fortunately, I knew the housekeeper there—a middle-aged, strong-minded woman, not easily frightened, which was a good thing. To her I communicated such information as I considered necessary. She consented to conceal me in the room where the safe stood. There was a cupboard close by the safe from which I could command a full view of the burglar's operations and pounce upon him at the right moment. If only my information was to be relied upon, there was every chance of my capturing the famous burglar.

Soon after midnight, when the house was all quiet, I went to the pantry and got into the cupboard, locking myself in. There were two openings in the panel, through either of which I was able to command a full view of the room. My position was somewhat cramped, but the time soon passed away. My mind was principally occupied in wondering if I was really about to have a chance of distinguishing myself. Somehow, there was an air of unreality about the events of the evening which puzzled me.

Suddenly I heard a sound which put me on the alert at once. It was nothing more than the creaking of a board or opening of a door would make in a quiet house; but it sounded intensified to my expectant ears. I drew myself up against the door of the cupboard and placed my eye to the opening in the panel. I had oiled the key of the door, and kept my fingers upon it in readiness to spring upon the burglar at the proper moment. After what seemed some time I saw the gleam of light through the keyhole of the door opening into the pantry. Then it opened, and a man carrying a small lantern came gently into the room. At first I could see nothing of his face; but when my eyes grew accustomed to the hazy light I saw that I had been rightly informed, and that the burglar was indeed no other than the famous Light Toed Jim.

As I stood there watching him I could not help admiring the cool fashion in which he went to work. He went over to the window and examined it. He tried the door of the cupboard in which I stood concealed. Then he locked the door of the pantry and turned his attention to the safe. He set his lamp on a chair before the lock and took from his pocket as neat and pretty a collection of tools as ever I saw. With these he went quietly and swiftly to work.

Light Toed Jim was a somewhat slimly built fellow, with little muscular development about him, while I am a big man with plenty of bone and sinew. If matters had come to a fight between us I could have done what I pleased with him; but I knew that Jim would not chance a fight. Somewhere about him I felt sure there was a revolver, which he would use on the least provocation. My plan, therefore, was to wait until his back was bent over the lock of the safe, then to open the cupboard door noiselessly and fall bodily upon him, pinning him to the ground beneath me.

Before long the moment came. He was working steadily away at the lock, his whole attention concentrated on the job. The slight noise of his drill was sufficient to drown the faint click of the key in the cupboard door. I turned it quickly and tumbled right upon him, driving the tool out of his hands and tumbling him into a heap at the foot of the safe. He uttered an exclamation of rage and astonishment as he went down, and immediately began to wriggle under me like an eel. As I kept him down with one hand I tried to pull out the handcuffs with the other. This somewhat embarrassed me, and the burglar profited by it to pull out a sharp knife. He had worked himself round on his back, and before I realized what he was after he was hacking furiously at me with his keen, dagger-like blade. Then I realized that we were going to have a fight for it, and prepared myself. He tried to run the knife into my side. I warded it off, but the blade caught the fleshy part of my left arm and I felt a warm stream of blood spurt out.

That maddened me, and I seized one of the steel drills lying near at hand, and hit my man such a blow over the temple that he collapsed at once, and lay as if dead. I put the handcuffs on him instantly, and, to make matters still more certain, I secured his ankles. Then I rose and looked at my arm. The knife had made a nasty gash, and the blood was flowing freely, but it was not serious; and when the housekeeper, who had just then appeared on the scene, had bandaged it, I went out and secured the help of the first policeman I met in conveying Light Toed Jim to the office.

I felt a proud man when I made my report to the inspector.

"Light Toed Jim?" said he. "What, James Bland? Nonsense, Parker." But I took him to the cells where Jim was being attended to by the doctor.

"You're right, Parker," he said. "That's the man. Well, this will be a fine thing for you."

After a time, feeling a little exhausted, I went home to try and get some sleep. The surgeon had attended to my arm, and told me it was but a superficial wound. It felt sore enough in spite of that.

I had no sooner reached my lodgings than I saw sitting in my easy-chair the strange man who had called upon me earlier in the evening. He rose to his feet when I entered. I stared at him in utter astonishment.

"Well, guv'nor," said he, "I see you've done it. You've got him square and fair, I reckon?"

"Yes," I said.

"Ah!" he said, with a sigh of complete satisfaction. "Then I'm satisfied. Yes, I don't know as how there's aught more I could say. I reckon as how Light Toed Jim an' me is quits."

I was determined to find out who this man was this time. "Sit down," I said. "There's a question or two I must ask you. Just let me get my coat off and I'll talk to you." I took my coat off and went over to the bed to lay it down. "Now then," I began, and looked around at him. I said no more, being literally struck dumb. The man was gone!

I began to feel uncomfortable. I ran hastily downstairs, only to find the outer door locked and bolted, as I had left it a few minutes before. I went back, utterly nonplussed. For an hour I pondered the matter over, but could neither make head nor tail of it.

When I went down to the office next morning I was informed that the burglar wanted to see me. I went to his cell, where he was lying in bed with his head bandaged. I had hit him pretty hard, as it turned out, and it was probable he would have to lie on the sick list for some days. "Well, guv'nor," said he, "you'd the best of me last night. You hit me rather hard that time."

"I was sorry to have to do it, my man," I answered. "You would have stabbed me if you could."

"Yes," he said, "I should. But I say, guv'nor, come a bit closer; I want to ask you a question. How did you know I was on that little job last night? For, s'elp me, there wasn't a soul knew a breath about it but myself. I hadn't no pals, never talked to anybody about it, never thought aloud about it, as I knows on. How came you to spot it, guv'nor?"

There was no one else in the cell with us, and I thought I might find out something about my mysterious visitor of the night before. "It was a pal of yours who gave me the information," I said.

"Can't be, guv'nor. No use telling me that. I ain't got no pals—leastways not in this job."

"Did you ever know a man like this?" I described my visitor. As I proceeded, Light Toed Jim's face assumed an expression of real terror. Whatever color there was in it faded away. I never saw a man look more thoroughly frightened. "Yes, yes," he said, eagerly. "In course I know who it is. Why, it's Barksea Bill, as I pal'd with at one time—and what did he say, guv'nor—that he owed me a grudge? That we was quits at last? Right you are, 'cos he did owe me a grudge. I treated Bill very shabby—very shabby, indeed, and he swore solemn he'd have his revenge. On'y, guv'nor, what you see wasn't Barksea Bill at all, but his ghost, 'cos Barksea Bill's been dead and buried this three year."

I was naturally very much exercised in my mind over this weird development of the affair, and I used to think about it long after Light Toed Jim had once more retired to the seclusion of Portland. While he was in charge at Westford I tried more than once to worm some more information out of him about the defunct Barksea Bill, but with no success. He would say no more than that "Bill was dead and buried this three year;" and with that I had to be content. Gradually I came to have a firm belief that I had indeed been visited by Barksea Bill's ghost, and I often told the story to brother officers, and sometimes got well laughed at. That, however, mattered little to me; I felt sure that any man who had gone through the same experience would have had the same beliefs.

Of course I got my promotion and was soon afterward married. Things went well with me, and I was lifted from one step to another. In my secret mind I was always sure I owed my first rise to the burglar's ghost, and I should have continued to think so but for an incident which occurred just five years after my capture of Light Toed Jim.

I had occasion to travel to Sheffield from Westford, and had to change trains at Leeds. The carriage I stepped into was occupied by a solitary individual, who turned his face to me as I sat down. Though dressed in more respectable fashion, I immediately recognized the man who had visited me so mysteriously at my lodgings. My first feeling was one of fear, and I daresay my face showed it, for the man laughed.

"Hallo, guv'nor," said he; "I see you knew me as soon as you come in. You owes a deal to me, guv'nor; now, don't you, eh?"

"Look here, my man," I said, "I've been taking you for a ghost these five years past. Now just tell me how you got in and out of my room that night, will you?"

He laughed long and loud at that. "A ghost?" said he. "Well, if that ain't a good un! Why, easy enough, guv'nor. I was a-lodging for a day or two in the same house. It's easy enough, when you know how, to open a door very quiet and to slip out, too."

"But I followed you sharp, and looked for you."

"Ay, guv'nor; but you looked down, and I had gone up! You should ha' come up to the attics, and there you'd ha' found me. So you took me for a ghost? Well, I'm blowed."

I told him what Light Toed Jim had said in the cell.

"Ay," said he, "I dessay, guv'nor. You see, 'twas this way—it weren't Jim's fault as I wasn't dead. He tried to murder me, guv'nor, he did, and left me a-lying for dead. So I ses to myself when I comes round that I'd pay him out sooner or later. But after that I quit the profession, Jim's nasty conduck havin' made me sick of it. So I went in for honest work at my old trade, which was draining and pipe repairing. I was on a job o' that sort in Westford, near Miss Singleton's house, when I see Light Toed Jim. I had a hidea what he was up to, havin' heard o' the plate, and I watches him one or two nights, and gets a notion 'ow he was going to work the job. Then, o' course, you being a officer and close at hand I splits on him—and that's all."

"But you had got the time and details correct?"

"Why, o' course, guv'nor. I was an old hand—served many years at Portland, I have, and I knew just how Jim would work it, after seeing his perlim'nary observations. But a ghost! Ha, ha, ha! Why, guv'nor, you must ha' been a very green young officer in them days!"

Perhaps I was. At any rate I learned a lesson from the ci-devant Barksea Bill—namely, that in searching a house it is always advisable to look up as well as down.

A PHANTOM TOE.

I AM not a superstitious man, far from it, but despite all my efforts to the contrary I could not help thinking, directly I had taken a survey of my chamber, that I should never quit it without going through a strange adventure. There was something in its immense size, heaviness and gloom that seemed to annihilate at one blow all my resolute skepticism as regards supernatural visitations. It appeared to me totally impossible to go into that room and disbelieve in ghosts.

The fact is, I had incautiously partaken at supper of that favorite Dutch dish, sauerkraut, and I suppose it had disagreed with me and put strange fancies into my head. Be this as it may I only know that after parting with my friend for the night I gradually worked myself up into such a state of fidgetiness that at last I wasn't sure whether I hadn't become a ghost myself.

"Supposing," ruminated I, "supposing the landlord himself should be a practical robber and should have taken the lock and bolt from off this door for the purpose of entering here in the dead of the night, abstracting all my property, and perhaps murdering me! I thought the dog had a very cutthroat air about him." Now, I had never had any such idea until that moment, for my host was a fat (all Dutchmen are fat), stupid-looking fellow, who I don't believe had sense enough to understand what a robbery or murder meant, but somehow or other, whenever we have anything really to annoy us (and it certainly was not pleasant to go to bed in a strange place without being able to fasten one's door), we are sure to aggravate it by myriads of chimeras of our own brain.

So, on the present occasion, in the midst of a thousand disagreeable reveries, some of the most wild absurdity, I jumped very gloomily into bed, having first put out my candle (for total darkness was far preferable to its flickering, ghostly light, which transformed rather than revealed objects), and soon fell asleep, perfectly tired out with my day's riding.

How long I lay asleep I don't know, but I suddenly awoke from a disagreeable dream of cutthroats, ghosts and long, winding passages in a haunted inn. An indescribable feeling, such as I never before experienced, hung upon me. It seemed as if every nerve in my body had a hundred spirits tickling it, and this was accompanied by so great a heat that, inwardly cursing mine host's sauerkraut and wondering how the Dutchmen could endure such poison, I was forced to sit up in bed to cool myself. The whole of the room was profoundly dark, excepting at one place, where the moonlight, falling through a crevice in the shutters, threw a straight line of about an inch or so thick upon the floor—clear, sharp and intensely brilliant against the darkness.

I leave you to conceive my horror when, upon looking at this said line of light, I saw there a naked human toe—nothing more.

For the first instant I thought the vision must be some effect of moonlight, then that I was only half awake and could not see distinctly. So I rubbed my eyes two or three times and looked again. Still there was the accursed thing—plain, distinct, immovable—marblelike in its fixedness and rigidity, but in everything else horribly human.

I am not an easily frightened man. No one who has traveled so much and seen so much and been exposed to so many dangers as I, can be, but there was something so mysterious and unusual in the appearance of this single toe that for a short time I could not think what to be at, so I did nothing but stare at it in a state of utter bewilderment.

At length, however, as the toe did not vanish under my steady gaze, I thought I might as well change my tactics, and remembering that all midnight invaders, be they thieves, ghosts or devils, dislike nothing so much as a good noise I shouted out in a loud voice:

"Who's there?"

The toe immediately disappeared in the darkness.

Almost simultaneously with my words I leaped out of bed and rushed toward the place where I had beheld the strange appearance. The next instant I ran against something and felt an iron grip round my body. After this I have no distinct recollection of what occurred, excepting that a fearful struggle ensued between me and my unseen opponent; that every now and then we were violently hurled to the floor, from which we always rose again in an instant, locked in a deadly embrace; that we tugged and strained and pulled and pushed, I in the convulsive and frantic energy of a fight for life, he (for by this time I had discovered that the intruder was a human being) actuated by some passion of which I was ignorant; that we whirled round and round, cheek to cheek and arm to arm, in fierce contest, until the room appeared to whiz round with us, and that at least a dozen people (my fellow traveler among them), roused, I suppose, by our repeated falls, came pouring into the room with lights and showed me struggling with a man having nothing on but a shirt, whose long, tangled hair and wild, unsettled eyes told me he was insane. And then, for the first time, I became aware that I had received in the conflict several gashes from a knife, which my opponent still held in his hand.

To conclude my story in a few words (for I daresay all of you by this time are getting very tired), it turned out that my midnight visitor was a madman who was being conveyed to a lunatic asylum at The Hague, and that he and his keeper had been obliged to stop at Delft on their way. The poor fellow had contrived during the night to escape from his keeper, who had carelessly forgotten to lock the door of his chamber, and with that irresistible desire to shed blood peculiar to many insane people had possessed himself of a pocketknife belonging to the man who had charge of him, entered my room, which was most likely the only one in the house unfastened, and was probably meditating the fatal stroke when I saw his toe in the moonlight, the rest of his body being hidden in the shade.

After this terrible freak of his he was watched with much greater strictness, but I ought to observe, as some excuse for the keeper's negligence, that this was the first act of violence he had ever attempted.

MRS. DAVENPORT'S GHOST.

BY FREDERICK P. SCHRADER.

DEAR readers, do you agree with Hamlet? Do you believe that there is more between heaven and earth than we dream of in our philosophy? Does it seem possible to you that Eliphas Levy conjured up the shade of Apollonius of Tyana, the prophet of the Magii, in a London hotel, and that the great sage, William Crookes, drank his tea at breakfast several days a week, for months in succession, in the society of the materialized spirit of a young lady, attired in white linen, with a feather turban on her head?

Do not laugh! Panic would seize you in the presence even of a turbaned spirit, and the grotesque spectacle would but intensify your terror. As for me, I did not laugh last night on reading an account in a New York newspaper of a criminal trial that will probably terminate in the death penalty of the accused.

It is a sad case. I shudder as I transcribe the records of the trial from the testimony of the hotel waiter, who heard the conversation of the two confederates through a keyhole, and of forty thoroughly credible witnesses, who testified to the same facts. What would be my feelings if I had seen the beautiful victim with the gaping wound in her breast, into which she dipped her finger to mark the brow of her murderer?

I.

About three o'clock on the afternoon of February 3, Professor Davenport and Miss Ida Soutchotte, a very pale and delicate young girl, who had submitted to the tests of Professor Davenport for a number of years, were finishing their dinner in their room in the second story of a New York hotel. Professor Benjamin Davenport was a celebrity, but it was said that he owed his fame to somewhat questionable means. The leading spiritualists did not repose the confidence in him that manifestly marked their regard for William Crookes or Daniel Douglas Home.

"Greedy and unscrupulous mediums," the author of Spiritualism in America thinks, "are to blame for the most bitter attacks to which our cause has been exposed. When the materializations do not take place as quickly as circumstances require, they resort to trickery and fraud to extricate themselves from a dilemma."

Professor Benjamin Davenport belonged to these "versatile" mediums. Aside from this, queer stories were afloat about him. He was secretly accused of highway robbery in South America, cheating at cards in the gambling houses of San Francisco, and the overhasty use of firearms toward persons who had never offended him. It was said almost openly, that the professor's wife had died from abuse and grief at his infidelity. But in spite of these annoying rumors, Mr. Davenport, by virtue of his skill as a fraud and fakir, continued to exercise a great deal of influence upon certain plain and simple-minded folks, whom it was impossible to convince that they had not touched the materialized spirits of their brothers, mothers, or sisters through the agency of his wonderful power. His professional success received material accession from his swarthy, Mephisto-like countenance, his deep, fiery eyes, his large curved nose, the cynical expression of his mouth, and the lofty, almost prophetic tone of his words.

When the waiter had made his last visit—he did not go far—the following conversation took place in the room:

"There is to be a seance this evening at the residence of Mrs. Harding," began the medium. "Quite a number of influential people will be there, and two or three millionaires. Conceal under your skirt the blonde woman's wig and the white material in which the spirits usually make their appearance."

"Very well," replied Ida Soutchotte, in a resigned tone.

The waiter heard her pace the room. After a pause, she asked:

"Whose spirit are you going to control this evening, Benjamin?"

The waiter heard a loud, brutal laugh and the chair groaning beneath the weight of the demonstrative professor.

"Guess."

"How should I know?" she asked.

"I am going to conjure up the spirit of my dead wife."

And another burst of laughter issued from the room, full of sinister levity. A cry of terror burst from Ida's lips. A muffled sound indicated to the eavesdropper at the door that she was dragging herself to the feet of the professor.

"Benjamin, Benjamin! don't do it," she sobbed.

"Why not? They say I broke Mrs. Davenport's heart. The story is damaging my reputation, but it will be forgotten if her spirit should address me in terms of endearment from the other shore in the presence of numerous witnesses. For you will speak to me tenderly, will you not, Ida?"

"No, no. You shall not do it; you shall not think of it. Listen to me, for God's sake. During the four years that I have been with you I have obeyed you faithfully and suffered patiently. I have lied and deceived, like you; I learned to imitate the sleep and symptoms of clairvoyants. Tell me, did I ever refuse to serve you, or utter a word of complaint, even when my shoulders bent with the weight of my burden, when you pierced the flesh of my arms with knitting needles? Worse than all this, I imitated distant voices behind curtains, and made mothers and wives believe that their sons and husbands had come from a better world to communicate with them. How often have I performed the most dangerous feats in parlors with the lamps turned low? Clothed in a shroud or white muslin I essayed to represent supernatural forms, whom tear-dimmed eyes recognized as those of departed dear ones. You do not know what I suffered at this unhallowed work. You scoff at the mysteries of eternity. I suffer the torments of an impending retribution. My God! if some time the dead whom I counterfeit should rise up before me with uplifted arms and dreadful imprecations! This constant terror has injured my heart— it will kill me. I am consumed by fever. Look how emaciated, how worn-out and downcast I am. But I am under your control. Do as you like with me; I am in your power, and I want it to be so. Have I ever complained? But do not force me to do this thing, Benjamin. Have pity on me for what I have done for you in the past, for what I am suffering. Do not attempt this mummery; do not compel me to play the role of your dead wife, who was so tender and beautiful. Oh, what put that thought into your mind? Spare me, Benjamin, I implore you!"

The professor did not laugh again. Amid the confusion of upturned articles of furniture the eavesdropper distinguished the sound of a skull striking the floor. He concluded that Professor Davenport had knocked Miss Ida down with a blow of his fist, or had kicked her as she approached him. But the waiter did not enter the room, as no one rang for him.

II.

That evening forty persons were assembled in Mrs. Joanne Harding's parlor, staring at the curtain where a spirit form was in process of materializing. One dark lantern in a corner of the room contributed the light that emphasized the darkness rather than relieved it. The room was pervaded by profound silence, save the quickened, suppressed breathing of the spectators. The fire in the grate cast mysterious rays of light, resembling fugitive spirits, upon the objects around, almost indistinguishable in the semi-gloom.

Professor Davenport was at his best this evening. The spirit world obeyed him without hesitation, like their lawful master. He was the mighty prince of souls. Hands that had no arms were seen picking flowers from the vases; the touch of an invisible spirit conjured sweet melodies from the keys of the piano; the furniture responded by intelligent rappings to the most unanticipated questions. The professor himself elevated his form in symbolical distortions from the floor to an altitude of three feet, indicated by

Mrs. Harding, and remained suspended in the air for a quarter of an hour, holding live coals in his hands.

III.

But the most interesting, as well as the most conclusive, test was to be the materialization of the spirit of Mrs. Arabella Davenport, which the professor had promised at the beginning of the seance.

"The hour has come," exclaimed the medium.

And while the hearts of all throbbed with anxious suspense, and their eyes distended with painful expectancy of the promised materialization, Benjamin Davenport stood before the curtain. In the twilight the tall man with the disheveled hair and demon look, was really terrible and handsome.

"Appear, Arabella!" he exclaimed, in a commanding voice, with gestures of the Nazarene at the sepulcher of Lazarus.

All are waiting——

Suddenly a cry burst from behind the curtain—a piercing, shuddering, horrible shriek, the shriek of an expiring soul.

The spectators trembled. Mrs. Harding almost fainted. The medium himself appeared surprised.

But Benjamin recovered his composure on seeing the curtain move and admit the spirit.

The apparition was that of a young woman with long blonde tresses; she was beautiful and pale, clad in some light, whitish material. Her breast was bare, and on the left side appeared a bleeding wound, in which trembled a knife.

The spectators arose and retreated, pushing their chairs to the wall. Those who chanced to look at the medium noticed that a deathly pallor had overspread his face, and that he was cowering and trembling.

But the young woman, Mrs. Arabella, the real one, whom he so well remembered, she had come in response to his summons, and advanced in a direct line toward Benjamin, who in terror covered his eyes to shut out the ghastly sight, and with a cry fled behind the furniture. But she dipped the finger of her thin hand into the blood from her wound and traced it across the brow of the unconscious medium, the while repeating, in a slow, monotonous tone that sounded like the echo of a wail, again and again:

"You are my murderer! You are my murderer!"

And while he was rolling and tossing in deadly terror on the floor they turned up the lights.

The spirit had vanished. But in the communicating room, behind the curtain, they found the body of poor Miss Ida Soutchotte with horribly distorted features. A physician who was present pronounced it heart stroke.

And that is the reason that Prof. Benjamin Davenport appeared alone in a New York courtroom to answer to the charge of having murdered his wife four years ago in San Francisco.

THE PHANTOM WOMAN.

HE took an all-possessing, burning fancy to her from the first. She was neither young nor pretty, so far as he could see—but she was wrapped round with mystery. That was the key of it all; she was noticeable in spite of herself. Her face at the window, sunset after sunset; her eyes, gazing out mournfully through the dusty panes, hypnotized the lawyer. He saw her through the twilight night after night, and he grew at length to wait through the days in a feverish waiting for dusk, and that one look at an unknown woman.

She was always at the same window on the ground floor, sitting doing nothing. She looked beyond, so the infatuated solicitor fancied, at him. Once he even thought that he detected the ghost of a friendly smile on her lips. Their eyes always met with a mute desire to make acquaintance. This romance went on for a couple of months.

Gilbert Dent assured himself that nothing in this life can possibly remain stationary, and he cudgeled his brain for a respectable manner of introducing himself to his idol.

He had hardly arrived at this point when he received a shock. There came an evening when she was not at the window.

Next morning he walked down Wood Lane on his way to the office. He always went by train, but he felt a strong disinclination to go through another day without a sight of her. His heart began to beat like a schoolgirl's as he drew near the house. If she should be at the window. He was almost disposed to take his courage in his hand and call on her, and—yes, even—tell her in a quick burst that she had mysteriously become all the world to him. He could see nothing ridiculous in this course; the possibility of her being married, or having family ties of any sort, had simply never occurred to him.

However, she was not at the window; what was more, there was a sinister silence, a sort of breathlessness about the whole place.

It was a very hot morning in late August. He looked a long time, but no face came, and no movement stirred the house.

He went his way, walking like a man who has been heavily knocked on the brow and sees stars still. That afternoon he left the office early, and in less than an hour stood at the gate again. The window was blank. He pushed the gate back—it hung on one hinge—and walked up the drive to the door. There were five steps—five steps leading up to it. At the foot he wheeled aside sharply to the window; he had a sick dread of looking through the small panes—why he could not have told.

When at last he found courage to look he saw that there was a small round table set just under the window—a work-table to all appearance; one of those things with lots of little compartments all round and a lid in the middle which shut over a well-like cavity for holding pieces of needlework. He remembered that his mother had one—thirty years before.

Round the edge of the table was gripped a small, delicate hand. Gilbert Dent's eyes ran from this bloodless hand and slim wrist to a shoulder under a coarse stuff bodice—to a rather wasted throat, which was bare and flung back.

So this was the end—before the beginning. He saw her. She was dead; twisted on the floor with a ghastly face turned up toward the ceiling, and stiff fingers caught in desperation round the work table.

He stumbled away along the path and into the lane.

For a long time he could not realize the horror of this thing. The influence of the decayed house hung over him—nothing seemed real. It was quite dark when he moved away from the gate, and went in the direction of the nearest police station. That she was dead—this woman whose very name he did not know although she influenced him so powerfully—he was certain; one look at the face would have told anyone that. That she was murdered he more than suspected. He had seen no blood about; there had been no mark on the long, bare throat, and yet the word rushed in his ears, "Murder."

Later on he went back with a police officer.

They broke into the house and entered the room. It was in utter darkness, of course, by now. Dent, his fingers trembling, struck a match. It flared round the walls and lighted them for a moment before he let it fall on the dusty floor.

The policeman began to light his lantern and turned it stolidly on the window. He had no reason for delay; he was eager to get to the bottom of the business. His professional zeal was whetted; this promised to be a mystery with a spice in it.

He turned the light full on the window; he gave a strange, choked cry, half of rage, half of apprehension. Then he went up to Gilbert Dent, who stood in the middle of the room with his hands before his eyes, and took his shoulder and shook it none too gently.

"There ain't nobody," he said.

Dent looked wildly at the window—the recess was empty except for the work-table. The woman was gone.

They searched the house; they minutely inspected the garden. Everything was normal; everything told the same mournful tale—of desertion, of death, of long empty years. But they found no woman, nor trace of one.

"This house," said the policeman, looking suspiciously into the lawyer's face, "has been empty for longer than I can remember. Nobody'll live in it. They do say something about foul play a good many years ago. I don't know about that. All I do know is that the landlord can't get it off his hands."

It was doubtful if Gilbert Dent heard one word of what the man was saying. He was too stunned to do anything but creep home—when he was allowed to go—and let himself stealthily into his own house with a latch key; he was afraid even of himself. He did not go to bed that night.

As for the mystery of the woman, the matter was allowed to drop; it ended—officially. There was a shrug and a grin at the police station. The impression there was that the lawyer had been drinking—that the dead woman in the empty room was a gruesome freak of his tipsy brain.

* * * * *

A week or so later Dent called on his brother Ned—the one near relation he had. Ned was a doctor; perhaps he was a shade more matter-of-fact than Gilbert; at all events, when the latter told his story of the house and the woman, he attributed the affair solely to liver.

"You are overworked"—the elder brother looked at the younger's yellow face. "An experience of this nature is by no means uncommon. Haven't you heard of people having their pet 'spooks'?"

"But this was a real woman," he declared. "I—I, well, I was in love with her. I had made up my mind to marry her—if I could."

Ned gave him a keen, swift glance.

"We'll go to Brighton to-morrow," he said, with quiet decision. "As for your work, everything must be put aside. You've run completely down. You ought to have been taken in hand before."

They went to Brighton, and it really seemed as if Ned was right, and that the woman at the window had been merely a nervous creation. It seemed so, that is, for nearly three weeks, and then the climax came.

It was in the twilight—she had always been part of it—that Gilbert Dent saw her again; the woman that he had found lying dead.

They were walking, the two brothers, along the cliffs.

The wind was blowing in their faces, the sea was booming beneath the cliff. Ned had just said it was about time they turned back to the hotel and had some dinner, when Gilbert with a cry leapt forward to the very edge of the flat grass path on which they were strolling. The movement was so sudden that his brother barely caught him in time. They struggled and swayed on the very edge of the cliff for a second; Gilbert, possessed by some sudden frenzy, seemed resolved to go over, but the other at last dragged him backward, and they rolled together on the close, thick turf.

At this point Gilbert opened his eyes and tried to get on his feet.

"Better?" asked his brother, cheerfully, holding out a helping hand. "Strange! The sea has that effect on some people. Didn't think that you were one of them."

"What effect?"

"Vertigo, my dear fellow."

"Ned," said the other solemnly, "I saw her. It is not worth your while to try to account for anything. I have been inclined to think that you were right—that she, the woman at the window, was a fancy, that I had fallen in love with a creation of my own brain; but I saw her again to-night. You must have seen her yourself—she was within a couple of feet of you. Why did you not try and save her? It was nothing short of murder to let her go over like that. I did my best."

"You certainly did—to kill us both," said Ned, grimly.

Gilbert gave him a wild look.

After luncheon Ned persuaded him to rest—watched him fall asleep, and then went out.

In the porch of the hotel he was met by a waiter on his return who told him that Gilbert had left about a quarter of an hour after he had himself gone out.

Directly he heard this he feared the worst; having, as is usual in such cases, a very hazy idea of what the worst might be. Of course he must follow without a moment's delay; but a reference to the time-table told him that there was not another train for an hour, and that was slow.

It was already getting dusk when he arrived there. He felt certain that Gilbert would go there. He got to the end of the lane and walked up it slowly, examining every house. There would be no difficulty in recognizing the one he wanted; Gilbert had described it in detail more than once.

He stood outside the loosely hanging gate at last, and stared through the darkness at the shabby stucco front and rank garden.

He went down a flight of steps to the back door, and finding it unfastened, stepped into a stone passage. It was one of the problems of the place that he should have avoided the main entrance door with a half-admitted dread, and that, only half admitting still, he was afraid to mount the long flight of stone stairs leading from the servants' quarters. However, he pulled himself together and went up to the room.

It was quite dark inside. He heard something scuttle across the floor; he felt the grit and dust of years under his feet. He struck a match—just as Gilbert had done—and looked first at the recess in which the window was built. The match flared round the room for a moment and gave him a flash picture of his surroundings. He saw the stripes of gaudy paper moving almost imperceptibly, like tentacles of some sea monster, from the wall; he saw a creature—it looked like a rat—scurry across the floor from the window to the great mantelpiece of hard white marble.

If he had seen nothing more than this.

He saw in detail all that the first match had flashed at him. He saw his brother lying on the floor; a ghastly coincidence, his hand was caught round the edge of the work-table as hers had been. The other hand was clenched across his breast; there was a look of great agony on his face.

A dead face, of course. This was the end of the affair. He was lying dead by the window where the woman had sat every night at dusk and smiled at him.

The second match went out; the brother of the dead man struck a third. He looked again and closely. Then he staggered to his feet and gave a cry. It rang through the empty rooms and echoed without wearying down the long, stone passages in the basement.

Gilbert's head was thrown back; his chin peaked to the ceiling. On his throat were livid marks. The doctor saw them distinctly; he saw the grip of small fingers; the distinct impression of a woman's little hand.

* * * * *

The curious thing about the whole story—the most curious thing, perhaps— is that no other eye ever saw those murderous marks. So there was no scandal, no chase after the murderer, no undiscovered crime. They faded; when the doctor saw his brother again in the full light and in the presence of others his throat was clear. And the post mortem proved that death was due to natural causes.

So the matter stands, and will.

But where the house and its overgrown garden stood runs a new road with neat red and white villas.

Whatever secret it knew—if any—it kept discreetly.

Ned Dent is morbid enough to go down the smart new road in the twilight sometimes and wonder.

THE PHANTOM HAG.

THE other evening in an old castle the conversation turned upon apparitions, each one of the party telling a story. As the accounts grew more horrible the young ladies drew closer together.

"Have you ever had an adventure with a ghost?" said they to me. "Do you not know a story to make us shiver? Come, tell us something."

"I am quite willing to do so," I replied. "I will tell you of an incident that happened to myself."

Toward the close of the autumn of 1858 I visited one of my friends, sub-prefect of a little city in the center of France. Albert was an old companion of my youth, and I had been present at his wedding. His charming wife was full of goodness and grace. My friend wished to show me his happy home, and to introduce me to his two pretty little daughters. I was feted and taken great care of. Three days after my arrival I knew the entire city, curiosities, old castles, ruins, etc. Every day about four o'clock Albert would order the phaeton, and we would take a long ride, returning home in the evening. One evening my friend said to me:

"To-morrow we will go further than usual. I want to take you to the Black Rocks. They are curious old Druidical stones, on a wild and desolate plain. They will interest you. My wife has not seen them yet, so we will take her."

The following day we drove out at the usual hour. Albert's wife sat by his side. I occupied the back seat alone. The weather was gray and somber that afternoon, and the journey was not very pleasant. When we arrived at the Black Rocks the sun was setting. We got out of the phaeton, and Albert took care of the horses.

We walked some little distance through the fields before reaching the giant remains of the old Druid religion. Albert's wife wished to climb to the summit of the altar, and I assisted her. I can still see her graceful figure as she stood draped in a red shawl, her veil floating around her.

"How beautiful it is! But does it not make you feel a little melancholy?" said she, extending her hand toward the dark horizon, which was lighted a little by the last rays of the sun.

The afternoon wind blew violently, and sighed through the stunted trees that grew around the stone cromlechs; not a dwelling nor a human being was in sight. We hastened to get down, and silently retraced our steps to the carriage.

"We must hurry," said Albert; "the sky is threatening, and we shall have scarcely time to reach home before night."

We carefully wrapped the robes around his wife. She tied the veil around her face, and the horses started into a rapid trot. It was growing dark; the scenery around us was bare and desolate; clumps of fir trees here and there and furze bushes formed the only vegetation. We began to feel the cold, for the wind blew with fury; the only sound we heard was the steady trot of the horses and the sharp clear tinkle of their bells.

Suddenly I felt the heavy grasp of a hand upon my shoulder. I turned my head quickly. A horrible apparition presented itself before my eyes. In the empty place at my side sat a hideous woman. I tried to cry out; the phantom placed her fingers upon her lips to impose silence upon me. I could not utter a sound. The woman was clothed in white linen; her head was cowled; her face was overspread with a corpse-like pallor, and in place of eyes were ghastly black cavities.

I sat motionless, overcome by terror.

The ghost suddenly stood up and leaned over the young wife. She encircled her with her arms, and lowered her hideous head as if to kiss her forehead.

"What a wind!" cried Madame Albert, turning precipitately toward me. "My veil is torn."

As she turned I felt the same infernal pressure on my shoulder, and the place occupied by the phantom was empty. I looked out to the right and left—the road was deserted, not an object in sight.

"What a dreadful gale!" said Madame Albert. "Did you feel it? I cannot explain the terror that seized me; my veil was torn by the wind as if by an invisible hand; I am trembling still."

"Never mind," said Albert, smiling; "wrap yourself up, my dear; we will soon be warming ourselves by a good fire at home. I am starving."

A cold perspiration covered my forehead; a shiver ran through me; my tongue clove to the roof of my mouth, and I could not articulate a sound; a sharp pain in my shoulder was the only sensible evidence that I was not the victim of an hallucination. Putting my hand upon my aching shoulder, I felt a rent in the cloak that was wrapped around me. I looked at it; five perfectly distinct holes—visible traces of the grip of the horrible phantom. I thought for a moment that I should die or that my reason should leave me; it was, I think, the most dreadful moment of my life.

Finally I became more calm; this nameless agony had lasted for some minutes; I do not think it is possible for a human being to suffer more than I did during that time. As soon as I had recovered my senses, I thought at first I would tell my friends all that had passed, but hesitated, and finally did not, fearing that my story would frighten Madame Albert, and feeling sure my friend would not believe me. The lights of the little city revived me, and gradually the oppression of terror that overwhelmed me became lighter.

So soon as we reached home, Madame Albert untied her veil; it was literally in shreds. I hoped to find my clothes whole and prove to myself that it was all imagination. But no, the cloth was torn in five places, just where the fingers had seized my shoulder. There was no mark, however, upon my flesh, only a dull pain.

I returned to Paris the next day, where I endeavored to forget the strange adventure; or at least when I thought of it, I would force myself to think it an hallucination.

The day after my return I received a letter from my friend Albert. It was edged with black. I opened it with a vague fear.

His wife had died the day of my return.

FROM THE TOMB.

TRANSLATED FROM THE FRENCH OF DE MAUPASSANT BY E. C. WAGGENER.

THE guests filed slowly into the hotel's great dining-hall and took their places, the waiters began to serve them leisurely, to give the tardy ones time to arrive and to save themselves the bother of bringing back the courses; and the old bathers, the yearly habitues, with whom the season was far advanced, kept a close watch on the door each time it opened, hoping for the coming of new faces.

New faces! the single distraction of all pleasure resorts. We go to dinner chiefly to canvass the daily arrivals, to wonder who they are, what they do and what they think. A restless desire seems to have taken possession of us, a longing for pleasant adventures, for friendly acquaintances, perhaps, for possible lovers. In this elbow-to-elbow life our unknown neighbors become of paramount importance. Curiosity is piqued, sympathy on the alert and the social instinct doubly active.

We have hatreds for a week, friendships for a month, and view all men with the special eyes of watering-place intimacy. Sometimes during an hour's chat after dinner, under the trees of the park, where ripples a healing spring, we discover men of superior intellect and surprising merit, and a month later have wholly forgotten these new friends, so charming at first sight.

There, too, more specially than elsewhere, serious and lasting ties are formed. We see each other every day, we learn to know each other very soon, and in the affection that springs up so rapidly between us there is mingled much of the sweet abandon of old and tried intimates. And later on, how tender are the memories cherished of the first hours of this friendship, of the first communion in which the soul came to light, of the first glances that questioned and responded to the secret thoughts and interrogatories the lips have not dared yet to utter, of the first cordial confidence and delicious sensation of opening one's heart to someone who has seemed to lay bare to you his own! The very dullness of the hours, as it were, the monotony of days all alike, but renders more complete the rapid budding and blooming of friendship's flower.

That evening, then, as on every evening, we awaited the appearance of unfamiliar faces.

There came only two, but very peculiar ones, those of a man and a woman—father and daughter. They seemed to have stepped from the pages of some weird legend; and yet there was an attraction about them, albeit an unpleasant one, that made me set them down at once as the victims of some fatality.

The father was tall, spare, a little bent, with hair blanched white; too white for his still young countenance, and in his manner and about his person the sedate austerity of carriage that bespeaks the Puritan. The daughter was, possibly, some twenty-four or twenty-five years of age. She was very slight, emaciated, her exceedingly pale countenance bearing a languid, spiritless expression; one of those people whom we sometimes encounter, apparently too weak for the cares and tasks of life, too feeble to move or do the things that we must do every day. Nevertheless the girl was pretty, with the ethereal beauty of an apparition. It was she, undoubtedly, who came for the benefit of the waters.

They chanced to be placed at table immediately opposite to me; and I was not long in noticing that the father, too, had a strange affection, something wrong about the nerves it seemed. Whenever he was going to reach for anything, his hand, with a jerky twitch, described a sort of fluttering zig-zag, before he was able to grasp what he was after. Soon, the motion disturbed me so much, I kept my head turned in order not to see it. But not before I had also observed that the young girl kept her glove on her left hand while she ate.

Dinner ended, I went out as usual for a turn in the grounds belonging to the establishment. A sort of park, I might say, stretching clear to the little station of Auvergne, Chatel-Guyon, nestling in a gorge at the foot of the high mountain, from which flowed the sparkling, bubbling springs, hot from the furnace of an ancient volcano. Beyond us there, the domes, small extinct craters—of which Chatel-Guyon is the starting point—raised their serrated heads above the long chain; while beyond the domes came two distinct regions, one of them, needle-like peaks, the other of bold, precipitous mountains.

It was very warm that evening, and I contented myself with pacing to and fro under the rustling trees, gazing at the mountains and listening to the strains of the band, pouring from the Casino, situated on a knoll that overlooked the grounds.

Presently, I perceived the father and daughter coming toward me with slow steps. I bowed to them in that pleasant Continental fashion with which one always salutes his hotel companions. The gentleman halted at once.

"Pardon me, sir," said he, "but may I ask if you can direct us to a short walk, easy and pretty, if possible?"

"Certainly," I answered, and offered to lead them myself to the valley through which the swift river flows—a deep, narrow cleft between two great declivities, rocky and wooded.

They accepted, and as we walked, we naturally discussed the virtue of the mineral waters. They had, as I had surmised, come there on his daughter's account.

"She has a strange malady," said he, "the seat of which her physicians cannot determine. She suffers from the most inexplicable nervous symptoms. Sometimes they declare her ill of a heart disease; sometimes of a liver complaint; again of a spinal trouble. At present they attribute it to the stomach—that great motor and regulator of the body—this Protean disease of a thousand forms, a thousand modes of attack. It is why we are here. I, myself, think it is her nerves. In any case it is sad."

This reminded me of his own jerking hand.

"It may be hereditary," said I, "your own nerves are a little disturbed, are they not?"

"Mine?" he answered, tranquilly. "Not at all, I have always possessed the calmest nerves." Then, suddenly, as if bethinking himself:

"For this," touching his hand, "is not nerves, but the result of a shock, a terrible shock that I suffered once. Fancy it, sir, this child of mine has been buried alive!"

I could find nothing to say, I was dumb with surprise.

"Yes," he continued, "buried alive; but hear the story, it is not long. For some time past Juliette had seemed affected with a disordered action of the heart. We were finally certain that the trouble was organic and feared the worst. One day it came, she was brought in lifeless—dead. She had fallen dead while walking in the garden. Physicians came in haste, but nothing could be done. She was gone. For two days and nights I watched beside her myself, and with my own hands placed her in her coffin, which I followed to the cemetery and saw placed in the family vault. This was in the country, in the province of Lorraine.

"It had been my wish, too, that she should be buried in her jewels, bracelets, necklace and rings, all presents that I had given her, and in her first ball dress. You can imagine, sir, the state of my heart in returning home. She was all that I had left, my wife had been dead for many years. I returned, in truth, half mad, shut myself alone in my room and fell into my chair dazed, unable to move, merely a miserable, breathing wreck.

"Soon my old valet, Prosper, who had helped me place Juliette in her coffin and lay her away for her last sleep, came in noiselessly to see if he could not induce me to eat. I shook my head, answering nothing. He persisted:

"'Monsieur is wrong; this will make him ill. Will monsieur allow me, then, to put him to bed?'

"'No, no,' I answered. 'Let me alone.'

"He yielded and withdrew.

"How many hours passed I do not know. What a night! What a night! It was very cold; my fire of logs had long since burned out in the great fireplace; and the wind, a wintry blast, charged with an icy frost, howled and screamed about the house and strained at my windows with a curiously sinister sound.

"Long hours, I say, rolled by. I sat still where I had fallen, prostrated, overwhelmed; my eyes wide open, but my body strengthless, dead; my soul drowned in despair. Suddenly the great bell gave a loud peal.

"I gave such a leap that my chair cracked under me. The slow, solemn sound rang through the empty house. I looked at the clock.

"It was two in the morning. Who could be coming at such an hour?

"Twice again the bell pulled sharply. The servants would never answer, perhaps never hear it. I took up a candle and made my way to the door. I was about to demand:

"'Who is there?' but, ashamed of the weakness, nerved myself and drew back the bolts. My heart throbbed, my pulse beat, I threw back the panel brusquely and there, in the darkness, saw a shape like a phantom, dressed in white.

"I recoiled, speechless with anguish, stammering:

"'Who—who are you?'

"A voice answered:

"'It is I, father.'

"It was my child, Juliette.

"Truly, I thought myself mad. I shuddered, shrinking backward before the specter as it advanced, gesticulating with my hand to ward off the apparition. It is that gesture which has never left me.

"Again the phantom spoke:

"'Father, father! See, I am not dead. Someone came to rob me of my jewels—they cut off my finger—the—the flowing blood revived me.'

"And I saw then that she was covered with blood. I fell to my knees panting, sobbing, laughing, all in one. As soon as I regained my senses, but still so bewildered I scarcely comprehended the happiness that had come to me, I took her in my arms, carried her to her room, and rang frantically for Prosper to rekindle the fire, bring a warm drink for her, and go for the doctor.

"He came running, entered, gazed a moment at my daughter in the chair—gave a gasp of fright and horror and fell back—dead.

"It was he who had opened the vault, who had wounded and robbed my child, and then abandoned her; for he could not efface all trace of his deed; and he had not even taken the trouble to return the coffin to its niche; sure, besides, of not being suspected by me, who trusted him so fully. We are truly very unfortunate people, monsieur."

He was silent.

Meanwhile the night had come on, enveloping in the gloom the still and solitary little valley; a sort of mysterious dread seemed to fall upon me in presence of these strange beings—this corpse come to life, and this father with his painful gestures.

"Let us return," said I, "the night has grown chill."

And still in silence, we retraced our steps back to the hotel, and I shortly afterward returned to the city. I lost all further knowledge of the two peculiar visitors to my favorite summer resort.

SANDY'S GHOST.

"'Commerdations fer the night, stranger? Waal, yes; I reckon we can fix a place fer you. Hev a cheer an' set you down."

"Thank you. Don't you find this rather a lonely place—no neighbors, no nothing, that I can see? How came you to settle here, so far removed from other habitations?"

"Waal, perhaps it's best not ter ask too many questions ter once."

"Beg your pardon. No offense was intended, I assure you. Simply idle curiosity."

"Don't say 'nuther word, stranger, but come in an' we'll hev a snack fer supper. Polly, bring on the victu'ls. Yer jes' in time."

Polly at once obeyed. She was a typical Western girl—tall, lithe, graceful and limpid-eyed. She was clear-skinned and high-spirited, too, and in this case ignorant through no fault of her own. John Barr's eyes scanned her intently, and a flush came to her cheeks. For the first time in her life she was unpleasantly conscious of her bare feet. It may have been this that made her stumble and spill some of the contents of an earthen bowl over the guest's knees as she placed it on the table.

Her eyes flashed and a tear of anger twinkled on the lashes. She stopped, half meaning to apologize, but an oath from her father caused her to set the bowl down heavily and to hurry from the cabin. A moment later Barr saw a flutter of pink calico from behind a pile of rocks. Old Kit Robinson saw it, too.

"Don't wonder at yer sayin' 'tain't right. She's a sma't gal, and a good looker, too, as should hev been sent away frum here ter school ter be eddicated. But she won't leave her no 'count dad. I orter be shot fer cussin' her. But I ain't what I use ter be. Settin' here an' keepin' guard makes me narvous."

Barr's eyes asked the question his lips refused to speak. Supper eaten, the men went outside and sat with their chairs tilted back against the cabin. Something in the younger man's frank face had softened old Kit into a reminiscent mood and made him strangely inclined to gratify an idle curiosity.

The soft evening winds sighed through the branches of the tall spruce pines, and the declining rays of the setting sun caused the shadow of the rude home to stretch out longer across the greensward. From its shelter where he sat John Barr looked out on the grand ranges of the Rockies and wondered where in their vastness he would find the man he sought—the finding of whom had brought him out into this wild and almost forsaken mining camp.

"Stranger, I've took a likin' ter you. Ye've a sumthin' about you thet reminds me of sum one I know, an' you look like an honest chap. Say, do you b'lieve in ghosts?"

He put the question very suddenly, and a look of disappointment crossed his face when Barr told him that he did not believe in spooks.

"Waal, I've seen 'em!"

A thought connecting the pink calico with something in the past came to Barr's mind.

"Can't you tell me about it?" he asked.

"I'd like ter if you'll sw'ar, on yer derringer, never ter blab. Will you sw'ar?"

The solitary guest started to smile, but the smile faded at the thought of unshed tears in Polly's eyes. It might make it easier for her if he humored the old man.

"I'll swear," he said. And he did.

"Do you see yan old spruce at the turn of the trail an' the cliff jes' above? Waal, thet's the spot I'm watchin' an' guardin' till the owner cums ter claim it. I'm quick ter burn powder an' a pretty sure shot. I know a man when I sees him, an' I ain't easy fooled. Waal, ter begin with, I had a pardner once, an' he wuz a man, sure 'nough. He wuz frum the State of New York. I never axed him as ter how so fine a gent cum ter be diggin' an' shov'lin' in the Rockies, though ter myself I said thar wuz sum good reason. He had light hair, an' we called him Sandy, fer short, an' he wuz jes' erbout as gritty as sand. We wuz as unlike as any two fellers you ever saw. He wuz quietlike an' steady, an' I wuz sorter wild an' reckless an' liked mounting dew mos' too well. Waal, when we had a little dust scraped together, we would divvy, an' I tuk my share way down ter the station on the other side of the cliffs an' sent it off ter the bank in Helena. But I allers left sum hid whar the gal would find it. Old Sandy hed a bank of his own thet no one knew erbout, 'cepting hisself, an' ev'ry time we divided he'd carry part of it ter his hidin' place, an' then give the rest ter me ter send ter his boy, thet he said wuz bein' eddicated in sum college way up in Boston. He seemed ter think a heap of thet boy. Arter awhile my old woman give out, an' soon we laid her away on the hillside. It wuz hard, stranger."

Old Kit's voice failed him for a moment, but he quickly regained his composure and continued:

"But when old Sandy, my good old pard, give up I didn't keer fer nothin'. We buried him in style. All the boys frum round the diggin's wuz thar, an' many an eye wuz wet. We didn't hev nary a preacher, but the gal she prayed at the grave. Fer the life of me I don't know where she larnt it. Reckon the old woman must hev told her. Next mornin' the gal showed me a letter thet Sandy give her jes' afore he died. It wuz ter his boy, an' she wuz ter give it ter him if he ever cum out this way, an' she's got it yet.

"Thet same evenin' after supper, feelin' kinder glumish an' like thar wuz sumthin' in my throat I couldn't swaller, I tuk a stroll up the gulch. I went on out ter the top of the edge of the big rock an' got ter studyin' whar I'd find another pard like Sandy. All ter once I felt a hand touch my shoulder kinder light once or twice. I jumped up, half expectin' it wuz Sandy, but it wuz only the gal. Waal, I wuz all tuk back at fust, an' then I got mad.

"'What air you doin' up here?' I axed, kinder rough. She hed tears in her eyes as she looked at me, an' said:

"'Pap, don't git mad. I wuz lonesum. I seed you cumin' up this way, an' I follered you, 'cause I wanted ter tell you thet Sandy said ter give his boy his pile when he cums.'

"'Waal,' says I, 'you might hev waited till I cum back ter the house.' An' then I sent her back.

"Arter she wuz gone I sot ter studyin' whar in the world Sandy's pile wuz. I tried ter think whar could he hev hid it. But it warn't no use. All ter once I noticed it wuz plum dark, an' as these mountings ain't a he'lthy place fer a man ter roam in arter nightfall, especially if he ain't got his shootin' irons on, I cut a pretty swift gait fer the shack.

"Jes' as I cum round the bend thar at the pine I happened ter look up terward the clift, an' thar sot Sandy. Yes, sir. It wuz him sure as yer born. My feet felt heavy as lead, an' I couldn't move frum the spot. I tried ter holler, but it warn't no go. Finally I gave a sudden jerk an' made a step terward him, an' as I did so he disappeared. Then I made tracks fer home. But I kept mum, 'cause I knowed the boys would say thet mounting dew wuz lickin' up my brains, an' I would be seein' snakes an' sich things afore long.

"The next night sumhow er 'nuther I thought ter go an' see if he wuz thar ag'in, an' sure 'nough, thar he sot, lookin' kinder sad an' making marks on the rocks with his fingers. I hed my hand on my gun this time, so I got a little closter than afore. But, by hookey, he got away from me ag'in, nor did he cum back.

"I could hardly wait fer the next night ter cum round. At the same time I wuz on hand good an' early, jes' as it begun ter git dark, an' the trees looked like long spooks a-stretchin' out their arms. I looked terward the clift, an' thar he sot a-markin' an' a-scratchin' on the rock with his fingers an' still looking sad.

Now, this bein' the third time, I kinder got bold, an' I went a little closter, an' says:

"'Sandy, wha-what's the ma-mat-matter with you? Didn't the boys do the plantin' right fer you?'

"Then as luck would hev it I thought of sumthin' else right quick, an' I said:

"'Or is it the dust you hev hid whar yer sittin'?'

"Waal, he looked up then, an' the happiest smile cum ter his face, an' all ter once he disappeared ag'in. An' since then I hev sot here an' guarded the place till the right one cums along ter claim it."

"Let's see. What did you say yer name wuz?"

"Pardon me. I thought I had told you. My name is John Willett Barr."

"Polly, oh, Polly! Cum hyar, gal. What wuz Sandy's full name? I plum fergot."

"What you want ter know fer?" she asked. "I ain't a-goin' ter tell you now. Thet's my own secret."

"Cum, cum, gal. Tell me ter once, or it won't be he'lthy fer you."

"Waal, then," she answered stubbornly, "it's John Willett Barr."

At her reply the younger man's face grew deathly pale, and he started up from his chair, but Kit thrust him back into his seat, saying:

"Bring me the letter, Polly."

"What are you goin' ter do with it, pa?" she inquired, cautiously.

"I promised old Sandy on my oath ter keep it till the right one cums erlong ter claim it, an' I mean ter keep my word. The right one is here, gal. Thar he sits. So trot thet letter out, an' don't parley long with me if you knows when yer well off."

Polly stared at the younger man in utter bewilderment for a moment. Then, turning slowly, she stepped quietly into the cabin after the precious document; an unusual gleam of joy lighted up her face and a suppressed excitement shone in her eyes. Under her breath she said: "Sumhow er ruther I felt he wuz the right one."

Too truly, John Barr realized in that painful moment that he whom he sought was now dead to him; that the father from whom he had been parted so many years was sleeping that long, dreamless sleep in the clay mound on the hillside, which marked his last resting place. As he turned to look at the face of old, honest Kit, who had been his father's friend during those long years of forced exile, a happy smile lit up the old miner's rugged features as he pointed with his finger to the rock cliff near the old spruce vine, and said, in an exultant, trembling voice:

"Thar he be, stranger—jes' as I hev seen him many a night—yer dad—my pard—pore old Sandy!"

With an eager voice John Barr sprang forward, and the mountains echoed and re-echoed the plaintive cry of "Father! Father!" But his outstretched arms clasped only emptiness and the darkening shadows of the rapidly approaching night.

THE GHOSTS OF RED CREEK.

BY S. T.

TO the northward of Mississippi City and its neighbor, Handsboro, there extends a tract of pine forest for miles with but few habitations scattered through it. Black and Red Creeks, with their numerous branches, drain this region into the Pascagoula River to the eastward. With the swamps of Pascagoula as a refuge, and the luxuriant and unfrequented bottoms of Red and Black Creeks to browse upon, there are few choicer spots for deer. Knowing this fact, a small party of gentlemen on the day before a crisp, cold Christmas, started from Handsboro in a large four-wheeled wagon for a thirty-mile drive into this wilderness of pine and a week's sport after the deer. The guide was Jim Caruthers, a true woodsman, and the driver and general factotum, a jolly negro named Jack Lyons, than whom no one could make a better hoe-cake and cook a venison steak. His laugh could be heard a quarter of a mile, and his good nature was as expansive as the range of the laughter.

The usual experiences of a hunting camp were heartily enjoyed during the first days of this life out of doors; but its cream did not rise until about the fifth night, when, from familiar intercourse, Jack Lyons became loquacious, and after the day's twenty or twenty-five-mile walk, would spin yarns in front of the camp fire, which brought forgetfulness of fatigue.

The night before New Year's was intensely cold. The cold north wind of the afternoon had subsided at sunset, and only a gust now and again touched the musical leaves of the pines, making them vibrant with that mournful score of nature's operas which even maestros have failed to catch.

In front of two new and white tents two sportsmen reclined at length within reach of the warmth of the fire, while opposite them rested at ease the guide and the worthy Jack Lyons.

Wearied with the day's chase four stanch hounds—Ringwood, Rose, Jet and Boxer—were dreaming of future quarry.

The firelight brought out in bright relief the trunks of the tall pines like cathedral columns, and sparkling through the leafy dome overhead the scintillating stars glistened with a diamond brightness. A silence which added its influence to the scene rested about the borders of the creek below, and gave more effect to the story of the veteran teamster than perhaps it otherwise would have had.

"If de deer run down de creek," said old Jack, smacking his lips over a carefully prepared brewing of the real Campbellton punch, "wese boun' to see fun to-morrer, for dey'll take us down thar by de old Gibbet's place. In daylight dere's no place like it, but after nightfall, you bet you wouldn't catch dis nigger thar."

Old Jack was naturally asked why he didn't care about visiting the Gibbet's place at night. Asking to be excused until he filled his pipe, the silence was unbroken until his return. He piled on more pine knots and commenced:

"You kno', gemmen, dat when de gunboats was in de sound we folks had to travel way back hyar on dese roads outun de range of deir big guns. I was 'gaged by Mr. Harrison in hauling salt from de factory at Mississippi City, on de beach ober to Mobile, an' I had been making a trip ebery week or so. Dis back country road was neber thought ob by de Federals, an' we had good times long de way, no shells and no shootin'.

"De nite, gemmen, I'se speakin' of was a Friday, dat yous all knows is unlucky. Well, you see, I hitched up Betsie an' Rose in de lead, an' ole Fox an' Blossom at de pole, an' takes in de biggest load of salt dat team eber carried. I starts out an' crosses de Biloxi Riber at Han'sboro jes' as de moon was goin' down. Yes, boss, dese roads weren't no better den now, an' de rain had made 'em mighty rough when yer come to de holes.

"I sat in de seat whistlin' 'De Cows is in de Pea Patch,' and a-thinkin' of Sarah Jamison, what was afterwards my wife, when I felt de off fore wheel go 'kersush' in a hole up to de hub. I'd made seventeen miles out ob Han'sboro. I did some cussin', an' den went to de fence, about twenty yards off, an' took out a rail to prize up de wheel. Den I saw I was at Mister Gibbet's place. I sez to myself, I'll go up to de house an' get old Mr. Gibbet to give me a turn. I had done gone by dar two weeks afore an' seed de old man.

"Now, gemmen, yer listen to me, for what I'se tellin' yer is as sure as Jinny'll blow de horn on de las' day. I walked up to de house an' dar I saw a bright light inside. It showed out froo de windows, an' I saw shadders of Miss Gibbet and Mrs. Gibbet on de window curtain—shore, honeys, shore. De front do' was shet, an' I steps up on ter de gallery an' knocks wid de butt end of my whip. I didn't knock loud, needer. God bless us all, gemmen, de lights went out like dat, an' I hears set up a laugh, ha-ha-ha-ha. How dat set my knees a-shakin'. I opens de do', an' dere was no sign of anybody. I struck a match an' all de furniture was moved out, an' de old red curtain dat I fought I seed was in rags. De whole family was gone, for shore. I didn't kno' 'zactly what to think 'bout dem strange voices, but I started back to de wagon, when it lightened, an' bress God, dar in de front yard was six graves jes' made. Somefin' wrong here, sed I; an' I builds a fire by de wagon an' digs de wheel out. Jes' den old Squire Pasture kem along de road from Mobile, an' he tells me de news. Ole man Gibbet cut de froats of his wife and fore chillerns an' shoot hisself in de head outun jealousy of his wife. Dey was all buried in de front yard, an' de house was deserted ten days befo'.

"Gemmen, when I hear dat, dem mules make de quickest time to Mobile eber seed; an' youse can tell me dar's no ghosts, but yo' don' catch me roun' dat log house of Gibbet's 'ceptin' sun's an hour high."

Jack looked suspiciously over his shoulder into the darkness and crawled into his blanket, muttering:

"It scares dis nigger eben now to tell 'bout dat night."

Sleep soon fell upon the camp, but the impression of old Jack's story survived the night, and the next day he still asserted its truth.

THE SPECTRE BRIDE.

THE winter nights up at Sault Ste. Marie are as white and luminous as the Milky Way. The silence that rests upon the solitude appears to be white also. Nature has included sound in her arrestment. Save the still white frost, all things are obliterated. The stars are there, but they seem to belong to heaven and not to earth. They are at an immeasurable height, and so black is the night that the opaque ether rolls between them and the observer in great liquid billows.

In such a place it is difficult to believe that the world is peopled to any great extent. One fancies that Cain has just killed Abel, and that there is need for the greatest economy in the matter of human life.

The night Ralph Hagadorn started out for Echo Bay he felt as if he were the only man in the world, so complete was the solitude through which he was passing. He was going over to attend the wedding of his best friend, and was, in fact, to act as the groomsman. Business had delayed him, and he was compelled to make his journey at night. But he hadn't gone far before he began to feel the exhilaration of the skater. His skates were keen, his legs fit for a longer journey than the one he had undertaken, and the tang of the frost was to him what a spur is to a spirited horse.

He cut through the air as a sharp stone cleaves the water. He could feel the tumult of the air as he cleft it. As he went on he began to have fancies. It seemed to him that he was enormously tall—a great Viking of the Northland, hastening over icy fiords to his love. That reminded him that he had a love—though, indeed, that thought was always present with him as a background for other thoughts. To be sure, he had not told her she was his love, because he had only seen her a few times and the opportunity had not presented itself. She lived at Echo Bay, too, and was to be the maid of honor to his friend's bride—which was another reason why he skated on almost as swiftly as the wind, and why, now and then, he let out a shout of exhilaration.

The one drawback in the matter was that Marie Beaujeu's father had money, and that Marie lived in a fine house and wore otter skin about her throat and little satin-lined mink boots on her feet when she went sledding, and that the jacket in which she kept a bit of her dead mother's hair had a black pearl in it as big as a pea. These things made it difficult—nay, impossible—for Ralph Hagadorn to say anything more than "I love you." But that much he meant to have the satisfaction of saying, no matter what came of it.

With this determination growing upon him he swept along the ice which gleamed under the starlight. Indeed, Venus made a glowing path toward the west and seemed to reassure him. He was sorry he could not skim down that avenue of light from the love star, but he was forced to turn his back upon it and face toward the northeast.

It came to him with a shock that he was not alone. His eyelashes were a good deal frosted and his eyeballs blurred with the cold, and at first he thought it an illusion. But he rubbed his eyes hard and at length made sure that not very far in front of him was a long white skater in fluttering garments who sped over the snows fast as ever werewolf went. He called aloud, but there was no answer, and then he gave chase, setting his teeth hard and putting a tension on his firm young muscles. But however fast he might go the white skater went faster. After a time he became convinced, as he chanced to glance for a second at the North Star, that the white skater was leading him out of his direct path. For a moment he hesitated, wondering if he should not keep to his road, but the strange companion seemed to draw him on irresistibly, and so he followed.

Of course it came to him more than once that this might be no earthly guide. Up in those latitudes men see strange things when the hoar frost is on the earth. Hagadorn's father, who lived up there with the Lake Superior Indians and worked in the copper mines, had once welcomed a woman at his hut on a bitter night who was gone by morning, and who left wolf tracks in the snow—yes, it was so, and John Fontanelle, the half-breed, could tell you about it any day—if he were alive. (Alack, the snow where the wolf tracks were is melted now!)

Well, Hagadorn followed the white skater all the night, and when the ice flushed red at dawn and arrows of lovely light shot up into the cold heavens, she was gone, and Hagadorn was at his destination. Then, as he took off his skates while the sun climbed arrogantly up to his place above all other things, Hagadorn chanced to glance lakeward, and he saw there was a great wind-rift in the ice and that the waves showed blue as sapphires beside the gleaming ice. Had he swept along his intended path, watching the stars to guide him, his glance turned upward, all his body at magnificent momentum, he must certainly have gone into that cold grave. The white skater had been his guardian angel!

Much impressed, he went up to his friend's house, expecting to find there the pleasant wedding furore. But someone met him quietly at the door, and his friend came downstairs to greet him with a solemn demeanor.

"Is this your wedding face?" cried Hagadorn. "Why, really, if this is the way you are affected, the sooner I take warning the better."

"There's no wedding to-day," said his friend.

"No wedding? Why, you're not——"

"Marie Beaujeu died last night——"

"Marie——"

"Died last night. She had been skating in the afternoon, and she came home chilled and wandering in her mind, as if the frost had got in it somehow. She got worse and worse and talked all the time of you."

"Of me?"

"We wondered what it all meant. We didn't know you were lovers."

"I didn't know it myself; more's the pity."

"She said you were on the ice. She said you didn't know about the big breaking up, and she cried to us that the wind was off shore. Then she cried that you could come in by the old French Creek if you only knew——?"

"I came in that way," interrupted Hagadorn.

"How did you come to do that? It's out of your way."

So Hagadorn told him how it came to pass.

And that day they watched beside the maiden, who had tapers at her head and feet, and over in the little church the bride who might have been at her wedding said prayers for her friend. Then they buried her in her bridesmaid's white, and Hagadorn was there before the altar with her, as he intended from the first. At midnight the day of the burial her friends were married in the gloom of the cold church, and they walked together through the snow to lay their bridal wreaths on her grave.

Three nights later Hagadorn started back again to his home. They wanted him to go by sunlight, but he had his way and went when Venus made her bright path on the ice. He hoped for the companionship of the white skater. But he did not have it. His only companion was the wind. The only voice he heard was the baying of a wolf on the north shore. The world was as white as if it had just been created and the sun had not yet colored nor man defiled it.

HOW HE CAUGHT THE GHOST.

"Yes, the house is a good one," said the agent; "it's in a good neighborhood, and you're getting it at almost nothing; but I think it right to tell you all about it. You are orphans, you say, and with a mother dependent on you? That makes it all the more necessary that you should know. The fact is, the house is said to be haunted——"

The agent could not help smiling as he said it, and he was relieved to see an answering smile on the two faces before him.

"Ah, you don't believe in ghosts," he went on; "nor do I, for that matter; but, somehow, the reputation of the house keeps me from having a tenant long at a time. The place ought to rent for twice as much as it does."

"If we succeed in driving out the ghost, you will not raise the rent?" asked the boy, with a merry twinkle in his eyes.

"Well, no—not this year, at any rate," laughed the agent. And so the house was rented; and the slip of a girl and the tall lad, her brother, went their way.

Within a week the family had moved into the house, and were delighted with it. It was large and cool, with wide halls and fine stairways, and with more room than they needed. But that did not matter in the least, for they had always been cramped in small houses, suffering many discomforts; and they never could have afforded such a place as this if it had not been "haunted."

"Blessings on the ghost!" cried Margaret, gaily, as she ran about as merry as a child. "Who would be without a ghost in the house, when it brings one like this?"

"And it is so near your school," said the mother; "and I used to worry so over the long walk; and David can come home to lunch now, and you don't know what a pleasure that will be."

"It seems to me," David gravely explained, "that if I should meet the ghost I would treat him with the greatest politeness and encourage him to stay. We shall not miss the room he takes, shall we? I think it would be well to set aside that room over yours, Maggie, for his ghostship's own, for we shall not need that, you know. Besides, the door doesn't shut, and he can go in and out without breaking the lock."

And then they all laughed and had a great deal of fun over the ghost, which was a great joke to them.

They were very tired that night and slept soundly all night long. When they met the next morning there was more laughter about the ghost which was shy about meeting strangers, probably, and had made no effort to introduce himself. For the next three days they were all hard at work, trying to bring chaos into something like order; and then it was time for the school to open, and Margaret was to begin teaching, and David inserted an advertisement in the city papers for a maid-of-all-work, who might help their mother in their absence.

For one whole day prospective colored servants presented themselves and announced:

"Is dis de house whar dey wants a worklady? No, ma'am, I ain' gwine to work in dis house. Ketch me workin' in no ha'nted house."

After which they each and all departed, and others came in their stead. One was secured after a while, but no sooner had she talked across the fence with a neighbor's servant than she, too, departed.

"Never mind, children," said Mrs. Craig, wearily, "I would much rather do the work than be troubled in this way."

So the maid-of-all-work was dismissed and the Craig family locked the doors and went to their rooms, worn out with the day's anxieties.

They had been in the house four days, and there had been neither sight nor sound of the ghost. The very mention of it was enough to start them all to laughing, for they were thoroughly practical people, with a fondness for inquiring into anything that seemed mysterious to them and for understanding it thoroughly before they let it go.

David was soon sleeping the sound sleep of healthy boyhood, and all was silent in the house, when Margaret stole softly into his room and laid her hand on his arm. He was not easy to waken, and several minutes had passed before he sat up in bed with an articulate murmur of surprise.

"Hush!" said Margaret, in a whisper, with her hand on his lips. "I want you to come into my room and listen to a sound that I have been hearing for some time."

"Doors creaking," suggested David, as he began to dress.

"Nothing of the kind," was all she said.

They walked up the stairway, and along the upper hall to the door of the unused room. Something was wrong with the lock and the door would not stay fastened, as I have said.

Something that was not fear thrilled their hearts as they pushed the door further ajar, and stood where they could see every foot of the vacant floor. One of their own boxes stood in the middle of the room, but aside from that, nothing was to be seen, and they looked at one another in silence.

"Hold the lamp a minute, Maggie," David said, at last, and then he went all over the room, and looked more particularly at its emptiness, and even felt the walls.

"Secret panels, you know," he said, with a smile, but it was a very puzzled smile indeed.

"I can't see what it could have been," Margaret said, as they went down the stairs.

"No, I can't see, either, but I'm going to see," said David. "That was a chain, and chains don't drag around by themselves, you know. A ghost could not drag a chain, if he were to try."

"The conventional ghost very often drags chains," said Margaret, as she closed the door of her room.

And then she lay awake all night and listened for the conventional ghost that dragged a chain, but it seemed that the weight of the chain must have wearied him, for he was not heard again.

The mother had slept through it all, and next morning they gave her a vivid account of the night's adventure.

"Perhaps it was someone in the house," she said, in alarm. There were no ghosts within the bounds of possibility, so far as she was concerned, but burglars were very possible, indeed.

Then Margaret and David both laughed more than ever.

"What fun it would be," said David, "for a burglar to get into this house and try to find something worth carrying away!"

So they went on to the next night, all three fully determined to spend the night in listening for the ghost, and running him to earth if possible.

But it was Margaret that heard the ghost, after all. She had been sleeping and was suddenly startled wide awake, and there, overhead, was the sound of the chain dragging; and just as she was on the point of springing out of bed to call her brother, the chain seemed to go out of the upper room. She lay still and listened, and in a moment she heard it again.

It was coming down the stairs.

There was no carpet on the stairs, and she could hear the chain drop from step to step, until it had come the whole way down. There it was, almost at the door of her room, and something that was strangely like fear kept her lying still, listening in horrified silence.

Then it went along the hall, dragging close to the door; and then further away; and back and forth for awhile; and then it began dragging back up the stairs again. Step by step she could hear it drawn over the edge of every step—and by the time it had reached the top she remembered herself and called David.

Again did the brother and sister make a tour of the upper room, with the lamp. Not only that, but they looked into every nook and corner of the upper part of the house, and at last came back, baffled. They had seen nothing extraordinary, and they had not heard a sound.

"I'm going to see that ghost to-night," David said to his sister the next evening.

"How?"

"I'm going to sit up all night at the head of the stairs. Don't say anything about it to mother; it might make her uneasy."

So, after the household were all quiet, David slipped into his place at the head of the stairs, and sat down to his vigil. He had placed a screen at the head of the stairway so that it hid him from view—as if a ghost cared for a screen—and he established himself behind it, and prepared to be as patient as he could.

It seemed to him that hours so long had never been devised as those the town clocks tolled off that night. He bore it until midnight moderately well, because, he argued with himself, if there were any ghosts about they would surely walk then; but they were not in a humor for walking; and still the hours rolled on without any developments. He took the fidgets, and had nervous twitches all over him, and at last he could endure it no longer, and had leaned his head back against the wall and was going blissfully to sleep when——

He heard a chain dragging just beyond the open door of that unused room.

In spite of himself a shiver ran down his back. There was no mistaking it; it was a real chain, if he had ever heard one. More than that, it had left the room, and was coming straight towards the stairs. The hall was dark, and it was impossible for him to see anything, although he strained his eyes in the direction of the sound. And even while he looked it had passed behind the screen, and was going down the stairs, dropping from step to step with a clank.

Half way down a narrow strip of moonlight from a stair-window lay directly across the steps. Whatever the thing was, it must pass through that patch of light, and David leaned forward and watched.

Down it went from step to step, and presently it had slipped through the light, and was down; and a little later it came back again, through the light, and up the stairs, and back into that unused room.

And then David slapped his knees jubilantly, and ran down to his room, and slept all the rest of the night.

Next morning he was very mysterious about his discoveries of the night before.

"Oh, yes, I saw the ghost," he said to Maggie. "There; don't ask so many questions; I'll tell you more about it to-morrow, maybe."

And that was all the information she could get from him. It was very provoking.

That day David made a purchase down town and brought home a bulky bundle, which he hid in his own room and would not let his sister even peep at.

"I'm going to try to catch a ghost to-night," he said, "and you know how it is; if I brag too much beforehand, I shall be sure to fail."

He was working with something in the hall after the others had retired; but he did not sit up this time. He went to bed, and Margaret listened at his door and found that he was soon asleep.

But away in the night they were all awakened by a squealing that brought them all into the hall in a great hurry; and there, at the head of the stairs, they found the huge rat-trap that David had set a few hours before, and in the midst of the toils was a rat.

"Why, David," exclaimed the mother, "I didn't know that there was a rat in the house."

And then, all at once, she saw that there was a long chain hanging from a little iron collar around the creature's neck, and she and Margaret cried together.

"And this was the ghost!"

Such a funny ghost when they came to think of it—this poor rat, with a nest in some hole of the broken chimney. He had been someone's pet, once, perhaps; and now, the households he had broken up, the nights he had disturbed, the wild sensations he had created—it made his captors laugh to think that this innocent creature had been the cause of the whole trouble.

"I'll get a cage for him, and take care of him for the rest of his life," said David. "We owe him so much that we can't afford to be ungrateful."

The next morning he took the ghost-in-a-cage and showed it to the agent, and gave him a vivid account of the capture.

"So, you have a good house for about half price, all on account of that rat," exclaimed the agent, grimly. "Young man—but never mind, you deserve it. What are you working for now? Six dollars a week? If you ever want to change your place—suppose you come around here. I think you need a business that will give you a chance to grow."

And the agent and David shook hands warmly over the cage of the "ghost."

GRAND-DAME'S GHOST STORY.

BY C. D.

I DON'T know whether you ever tell your children ghost stories or not; some mothers don't, but our mother, though of German descent, was strong-minded on the ghost subject, and early taught all of her children to be fearless mentally as well as physically, and, though dearly fond of hearing ghost stories, especially if they were real true ghosts, we were sadly skeptical as to their being anything of the kind that could harm. We were quite learned in ghostly lore, knew all about "doppeigangers," "Will o' the Wisp," "blue lights," etc., and we could not have a greater treat for good behavior than for our mother to draw on her store of supernatural tales for our entertainment. The story I am about to relate she told us one stormy night, when, gathered round her chair in her own cozy sanctum, before a cheerful fire, we ate nuts and apples, and listened while she recited "an o'er true tale," told her by her grandmother, who herself witnessed the vision:

It was a fearful night, the wind sobbed and wailed round the house like lost spirits mourning their doom; the rain beat upon the casements, and the trees, writhing in the torture of the fierce blast, groaned and swayed until their tops almost swept the earth; bright flashes of lightning pierced even through the closed shutters and heavy curtains, and the thunder had a sullen, threatening roar that made your blood creep. It was a night to make one seek to shut out all sound, draw the curtains close, stir the fire and nestle deep in the arm-chair before it, with feet upon the fender, and have something cheerful to think or talk about. But I was all alone; none in the house with me but the servants, and the servants' wing was detached from the main part of the building, for I do not care to have menials near me, and I had no loved ones near.

It was just such a night that Nancy Black died. "What a fearful night for the soul to leave its earthly home and go out into the vast, unknown future!" I spoke aloud, as, rousing from a train of thought, I drew my heavy mantle closer round me, wheeled my arm-chair nearer the fire, and cuddled down in it, burying my feet in the foot-cushion to warm them, for I felt strangely cold. I was in the library; it was my usual sitting-room, for I seldom used the parlors. What was the use? My books were my friends, and I loved best to be with them. My children dead, or married and away, the cold, grand parlors always seemed gloomy and sad; the ghosts of departed pleasures haunted them, and I cared not to enter them.

It was a long, wide room across the hall from the parlors, running the whole length of the house, and was lined with shelves from floor to ceiling. My husband's father had been a bibliomaniac, and my husband had had a leaning that way also, and the shelves held many an old rare work that was worth its weight in gold. The fire, though burning brightly, did not illume one-half the room of which, sitting in the chimney corner, I commanded a full view, and had been looking at the shadows playing on the furniture and shelves, as the flame shot up, and after flickering a moment, would die out, leaving a gloom which would break away into fantastic shadows as the firelight would again shoot up.

While watching the gleams of light and darkling shades, unconsciously the wailing of the storm outside attracted my attention, there seemed to be odd noises of tapping on the windows, and sobs and sighs, as though someone was entreating entrance from the fierce tumult; and as I sat there, again I thought of Nancy Black, the old schoolgirl friend who had loved me so dearly, and the night when she went forth to meet the doom appointed her; resting my head upon my hand, I sat gazing in the fire, thinking over her strange life, and still stranger death, and wondering what could have become of the money and jewels that I knew she had once possessed.

While sitting thus, a queer sensation crept over me; it was not fear, but a feeling as though if I'd look up I'd see something frightful; a shiver, not like that of cold, ran from my head to my feet, and a sensation as though someone was breathing icy cold breath upon my forehead, the same feeling you would cause by holding a piece of ice to your cheek; it fluttered over my face and finally settled round my lips, as though the unseen one was caressing me, thrilling me with horror. But I am not fearful, nervous nor imaginative, and resolutely throwing off the dread that fell upon me, I turned round and looked up, and there, so close by my side that my hand, involuntarily thrown out, passed through her seeming form, stood Nancy Black. It was Nancy Black, and yet not Nancy Black; her whole body had a semi-transparent appearance, just as your hand looks when you hold it between yourself and a strong light; her clothing, apparently the same as worn in life, had a wavy, seething, flickering look, like flames have, and yet did not seem to burn.

"In the name of God, Nancy Black, what brought you here, and whence came you?" I exclaimed.

A hollow whisper followed:

"Thank you, my old friend, for speaking to me, and, oh, how deeply I thank you for thinking of me to-night—I shall have rest."

Rest! I heard echoed, and a jeering laugh rang through the room that made her quiver at its sound.

"I have been near you often; but always failed to find you in a condition when you would be en rapport before to-night. What I came for I will tell you;

whence I come, you need not know; suffice it to say, that were I happy I would not be here on such an errand, nor on such a night—it is only when the elements are in a tumult, and the winds wail and moan, that we come forth. When you hear these sounds it is souls of the lost you hear mourning their doom—'tis then they wander up and down, to and fro, their only release from their fearful home of torture and undying pain.

"I have come to tell you that you must go over to the old house, and in the back room I always kept locked, have the carpet taken up from toward the fireplace. You will see a plank with a knot-hole in it. Remove that, and you will find what caused me to lose my soul—have prayers said for me, for 'tis well to pray for the dead. The money and jewels give in charity; bury in holy ground the others you find, and pray for them and me. Ah! Jeannette, you thought your old friend, though strange and odd, pure and innocent. It is a bitter part of my punishment that I must change your thought of me. Farewell! Do not fail me, and I shall trouble you no more. But whenever you hear that wind howl and sweep round the house as it does to-night, know that the lost are near. It is their swift flight through space—fleeing before the scourge of memory and conscience—that causes that sound.

"That to-morrow you may not think you are dreaming, here is a token," and she touched the palm of my hand with her finger-tips, and as you see, my child, to this day, there are three crimson spots in the palm of my hand that nothing will eradicate.

"Do not fail me, and pray for us, Jeannette, pray," and with a longing, wistful gaze, and a deep, sobbing sigh, Nancy Black faded from my sight.

"Am I dreaming?" I exclaimed, as I rose from my chair and rang the bell. When the servant entered, I bade him attend to the fire and light the lamps, and I went through the room to see if any unusual arrangement of the furniture could have caused the appearance, but nothing was apparent, and I bade him send my maid to attend me in my chamber, for I could not help feeling unwilling to remain in the library any longer that evening.

While making my toilet for the night my maid said:

"Have you burned your hand, madam?"

Glancing hastily down, I saw three dark crimson spots upon the palm of my left hand. They had an odd look, seared as though touched by a red-hot iron, yet the flesh was soft, not burned and not painful. Making some excuse for it, I did not allude to it again, and dismissed her speedily, that I might reflect undisturbed over the singular occurrence. There were the marks upon my hand; I could not remove them, and they did not fade. In fact, their deep red made the rest of the palm lose its pinkish hue and look pale from the strong contrast. Could I have been asleep and dreamed it all, and by any means have done this to myself? I thought, but finally concluded that on the morrow I'd go over to Nancy Black's old residence and settle the question; and with that conclusion had to content myself until the morrow came.

Nancy Black was an old friend from my girlhood, who had owned large property in the town, and lived all alone in a spacious stone house directly opposite my home, and who, when dying, had left me the sole legatee of her property.

When morning came I took the keys, and, with my maid, went over to Nancy's house. It had never been disturbed since her death, which was sudden and somewhat singular, and the furniture remained just as she left it when taken to her last resting place. We went to the room Nancy had directed. I bade Sarah take up the carpet, and, sure enough, there was a plank with a knot-hole in it; so I sent her from the room, and lifted the plank myself, and there, between the two joints, rested a long box, the lid not fastened. Opening it, I was horrified to see two skeletons—those of an infant and of a woman, small in stature and delicate frame. In a moment it flashed before me that I saw all that remained of Nancy Black's young sister, a girl of seventeen, who had left home somewhat mysteriously years ago, and had died while absent—at least, that was the version Nancy had given of her absence, and no one had dreamed of doubting it, her tale was so naturally told.

Left orphans when Lucy was only two years and Nancy eighteen, she had devoted her life to the care of this young girl, and when she found her sister had fallen, she, in her pride of name and position, had destroyed mother and child, that her shame might not be known, and had lived all those dreary years in that house with her fearful secret.

Round the box, heaped up on every side, were money and jewels, and a parchment scroll among them had written on it: "Lucy's share of our father's estate." I carried out Nancy's wishes to the letter, for I now firmly believed that she had come to me herself that night. To avoid scandal resting on the dead, I took our clergyman into my confidence, and with his assistance had the remains buried quietly in consecrated ground. The money and jewels were given to the poor, and the old building I turned into a home for destitute females; and morning and night, as I kneel in prayer, I pray forgiveness to rest upon Nancy Black and peace to her troubled soul.

A FIGHT WITH A GHOST.

BY Q. E. D.

"No, I never believed much in ghosts," said the doctor. "But I was always rather afraid of them."

"Have you ever seen one?" asked one of the other men.

The doctor took his cigar out of his mouth and contemplated the ash for a moment or two before replying. "I have had some rather startling experiences," he said, after a pause, during which the rest of us exchanged glances, for the doctor has seen many things and is not averse to talking about them in congenial company. "Would you care about hearing one of them? It gives me the cold shivers now to speak of it." We nodded, and the doctor, taking a sip as an antidote to the shivers, began:

"You remember George Carson, who played for the 'Varsity some years ago; big chap, with a light mustache? Well, I saw a good deal of him before he married, while he was reading for the bar in town. It was just after he became engaged to Miss Stonor, who is now Mrs. Carson, that he asked me to go down to a place which his people had taken in the country. Miss Stonor was to be there and he wanted me to meet her. I could not go down for Christmas Day, as I had promised to be with my people. But as I had been working a bit too hard, and wanted a few days' rest, I decided to run down for a few days about the New Year.

"Woodcote was a pleasant enough place to look at. There were two packs of hounds within easy distance, and it was not far enough from a station to cut you off completely from the morning papers. The Carsons had been lucky, I thought, in coming across such a good house at such a moderate figure. For, as George told me, the owner had been obliged to go abroad for his health, and was anxious not to leave the place empty all the winter. It was an old house, with big gables and preposterous corners all over the place, and you couldn't walk ten paces along any of the passages without tumbling up or down stairs. But it had been patched from time to time and, among other improvements, a big billiard-room had been built out at the back. A country house in the winter without a billiard-room, when the frost stops hunting, is just—well, not even a gilded prison. The party was a small one; besides George and his father and mother, there were only a couple of Misses Carson, who, being somewhere in the early teens, didn't count, and Miss Stonor, who, of course, counted a good deal, and, lastly, myself.

"Miss Stonor ought to have been happy, for George Carson, besides being an excellent fellow all around, was by no means a bad match, being an only son with considerable expectations. But, somehow or other, she did not strike me as looking either very well or very happy. She gave me the impression of having something on her mind, which made her alternately nervous and listless. George, I fancied, noticed it, and was puzzled by it, for I caught him several times watching her with an anxious and inquiring look, but, as I was not there as a doctor, of course it was no business of mine, though I discovered the reason before I left Woodcote.

"The second night after my arrival—we had been playing, I remember, a family pool; the rest had gone upstairs to bed—George and I adjourned to a sort of study, which he had arranged upstairs, for a final smoke and a chat before turning in. The study was next to his bedroom, and parted off from it by curtains. As we were settling down I missed my pipe, and remembered that I had laid it down in the billiard-room. On principle I never smoke another man's pipe, so I lit a candle, the house being in darkness, and started away in search of my own. The house looked awfully weird by the flickering light of a solitary candle, and the stairs creaked in a particularly gruesome way behind me, just for all the world as though someone were following at my heels. I found my pipe where I had expected in the billiard-room, and came back in perhaps a little more hurry than was absolutely necessary. Which, perhaps, explains why I stumbled in the uncertain light over a couple of unforeseen stairs, and dropped my candle. Of course it went out, but after a little groping I found it. Having no matches with me I was obliged to feel my way along the banisters, for it was so dark that I could not see my hand in front of me. And as I slowly advanced, sliding my hand along the broad balustrade at my side, it suddenly slid over something cold and clammy, which was not balustrade at all; for, stopping dead, and closing my fingers round it for an instant, I felt that I was holding another hand, a skinny, bony hand, which writhed itself slowly from my grasp. And though I could hear nothing and see nothing, I was yet conscious that something was brushing past me and going up the stairs.

"'Hi—what's that? Who are you?' I called.

"There was no answer.

"I admit that I was in a regular funk. I must have shown it in my face.

"'What's the matter?' asked George, as I blundered into his study.

"'Oh, nothing,' I answered; 'dropped my candle and lost the way.'

"'But who were you talking to?'

"'I was only swearing at the candle,' I replied.

"'Oh! I thought perhaps you had seen—somebody,' replied George.

"Somehow I did not like to tell him the truth, for fear he would laugh at my nervousness. But I determined to keep an eye on my liver, and take a couple of weeks' complete rest. That night I woke up several times with the feeling of that confounded hand under my own—a clammy hand which writhed as my fingers closed upon it.

"The next morning after breakfast I was in the billiard-room practicing strokes while Carson was over at the stables. Presently the door opened, and Miss Stonor looked in.

"'Come in,' I said; 'George will be back from the stables in a few minutes. Meanwhile we can have fifty up.'

"'I wanted to speak to you,' she said.

"She was looking very tired and ill, and I began to think I should not have an uninterrupted holiday after all.

"'Do you believe in ghosts?' she asked, having closed the door and come up to the table, where she stood leaning with both her hands upon it.

"'No,' I replied, missing an easy carrom as I remembered my experience of last night, 'but I believe in fancy.'

"'And, supposing then that a person fancied he saw things, is there any remedy?'

"'What do you mean, Miss Stonor?' I replied, looking at her in some surprise. 'Do you mean that you fancy——'

"I stopped, for Miss Stonor turned away, sat down on one of the easy-chairs by the wall, and burst into tears.

"'Oh! please help me' she sobbed; 'I believe I am going mad.'

"I laid down my cue and went over to her.

"'Look here, Miss Stonor,' I said, taking her hand, which was hot and feverish, 'I am a doctor, and a friend of George. Now tell me all about it, and I'll do my best to set it right.'

"She was in a more or less hysterical condition, and her words were freely punctuated by sobs. But gradually I managed to elicit from her that nearly every night since she came to Woodcote she had been awakened in some mysterious way, and had seen a horrible face looking at her from over the top of a screen which stood by the door of her bedroom. As soon as she moved the face disappeared, which convinced her that the apparition existed only in her imagination. That seemed to distress her even more than if she had believed it to be a genuine ghost, for she thought her brain was giving way.

"I told her that she was only suffering from a very common symptom of nervous disorder, as indeed it was, and promised to send a groom into the village to get a prescription made up for her. And, having made me promise to breathe no word to anyone on the subject, more especially to George, she went away relieved. Nevertheless, I was not quite certain that I had made a correct diagnosis of the case. You see I had been rather upset myself not many hours before. George was longer than I expected at the stable, and I was just going to find him when at the door I met Mrs. Carson.

"'Can you spare me one moment?' she said, as I held open the door for her. 'I wanted to find you alone.'

"'Certainly, Mrs. Carson, with pleasure; an hour, if you wish,' I replied.

"'It is so convenient, you know, to have a doctor in the house,' she said, with a nervous laugh. 'Now I want you to prescribe me a sleeping draught. My nerves are rather out of order, and—I don't sleep as I should.'

"'Ah,' I said, 'do you see faces—and such like things when you wake?'

"'How do you know?' she asked quickly.

"'Oh, I inferred from the other symptoms. We doctors have to observe all kinds of little things.'

"'Well, of course, I know it is only fancy; but it is just as bad as if it were real. I assure you it is making me quite ill; and I didn't like to mention it to Mr. Carson or to George. They would think I was losing my head.'

"I gave Mrs. Carson the same prescription as I had written for Miss Stonor, though by that time the conviction had grown upon me that there was something wrong which could not be cured by medicine. However, I decided to say nothing to George about the matter at present. For I could hardly utilize the confidence which had been placed in me by Miss Stonor and Mrs. Carson. And my own experience of the night before would scarcely have appeared convincing to him. But I determined that on the next day—which was Sunday—I would invent an excuse for staying at home from church and make some explorations in the house. There was obviously some mystery at work which wanted clearing up.

"We all sat up rather late that night. There seemed to be a general disinclination to go to bed. We stayed all together in the billiard-room until nearly midnight, and then loitered about in the hall, talking in an aimless sort of fashion. But at last Mrs. Carson said good-night, with a confidential nod to me, and Miss Stonor murmured, 'So many thanks; I've got it,' and they both went upstairs. George and I parted in the corridor above. Our rooms were opposite each other.

"I did not begin undressing at once, but sat down and tried to piece together some theory to account for the uncanniness of things. But the more I thought, the more perplexing it became. There was no doubt whatever that I had put my hand on something extremely alive and extremely unpleasant the night before. The bare recollection of it made me shudder. What living thing could possibly be creeping about the house in the dark? It was a man's hand. Of that I was certain from the size of it. George Carson was out of the question, for he was in his room all the time. Nor was it likely that Mr. Carson, senior, would steal about his own house in his socks and refuse to answer when spoken to. The only other man in the house was an eminently respectable-looking butler; and his hand, as I had noted particularly when he poured out my wine at dinner, was plump and soft, whereas the mysterious hand on the balustrade was thin and bony. And then, what was the real explanation of the face which had appeared to the two ladies? Indigestion might have explained either singly. Extraordinary coincidences do sometimes occur, but it seemed too extraordinary that a couple of ladies—one old and one young—should suffer from the same indigestion in the same house, at the same time, and with the same symptoms. On the whole, I did not feel at all comfortable, and looked carefully in all the cupboards and recesses, as well as under the bed, before starting to undress. Then I went to the door, intending to lock it. Just as my hand was upon the key, I heard a soft step in the corridor outside, accompanied by a sound which was something between a sigh and a groan. Very faint, but quite unmistakable, and, under the circumstances, discomposing. It might, of course, be George. Anyhow, I decided to look and see. I turned the handle gently and opened the door. There was nothing to be seen in the corridor. But on the opposite side I could see a door open, and George's head peeping round the corner.

"'Hullo!' he said.

"'Hullo!' I replied.

"'Was that you walking up the passage?' he asked.

"'No,' I answered, 'I thought it might be you.'

"'Then who the devil was it?' he said. 'I'll swear I heard someone.'

"There was silence for a few moments. I was wondering whether I had better tell him of the fright I had already had, when he spoke again:

"'I say, just come here for a bit, old fellow; I want to speak to you.'

"I stepped across the passage, and we went together into the little study which adjoined his bedroom.

"'Look here,' he said, poking up the fire, which was burning low, 'doesn't it strike you that there is something very odd about this house?'

"'You mean——'

"'Well, I wouldn't say anything about it to the master or Miss Stonor for fear of frightening them. All the same, scarcely a night passes but I hear curious footsteps on the stairs. You've heard them yourself, haven't you?'

"'Now you mention it,' I said, 'I confess I have.'

"'And, what is more,' he continued, 'I was sitting here two nights ago half asleep, and—it seems ridiculous, I know, but it's a fact—I suddenly saw a horrible face glaring at me from between those curtains behind you. It was gone in a moment, but I saw it as plainly as I see you.'

"I moved my seat uneasily.

"'Did you look in your bedroom or in the passage?' I asked.

"'Yes—at once,' he replied. 'There was nothing to be seen; but twice again that night I heard footsteps passing—good God!'

"He started up in his chair, staring straight over my shoulder. I turned quickly and saw the curtains which parted off the bedroom swing together.

"'What is it?' I asked, breathlessly.

"'I saw it again—the same face—between the curtains.'

"I tore the hangings aside, and rushed into the next room. It was empty. The lamp was burning upon a side table, and the door was open, just as George had left it. In the passage outside all was quiet. I came back into the study and found George running his fingers through his hair in perplexity.

"'There is clearly one person too many in the house,' I said. 'I think we ought to draw the place and find out who it is.'

"'All right,' said he, picking up the poker from the fireplace; 'if it's anything made of flesh and blood this will be useful, and if not——'

"He stopped short, for at that instant the most awful shriek of horror rang through the house—a shriek of wild, uncontrollable terror, such as I had never heard before and I never hope to hear again. One moment we stood staring at each other, dumbfounded. The next George Carson had dashed out of the room and down the corridor to the stairs. I followed close behind him. For we both knew that none but a woman in mortal fear would shriek like that, and that that woman was Miss Stonor.

"Down the stairs we tumbled pell-mell in the darkness. But before I reached the landing below, where Miss Stonor's room was, I felt, as I had felt the evening before, something brush swiftly past me. As I ran I turned and caught at it in the dark. But my hand gripped only empty air. I was just about to turn back and follow it, when a cry from George arrested me, and, looking down, I saw him standing over the prostrate form of Miss Stonor. The door of her room was open, and by the moonlight which streamed into the room I could see her lying in her white nightdress across the threshold. What followed in the next few minutes I can scarcely recall with accuracy. The whole house was aroused by the poor girl's awful shriek. She was quite unconscious when we came upon her, but she revived more or less as soon as Mrs. Carson and one of the terrified servants had lifted her into bed again. Nothing intelligible could be gathered from her, however, as to the cause of her fright; she only repeated, hysterically, again and again:

"'Oh, the face; the face!'

"When I saw I could do her no further good for the present, I took George by the arm and led him out of the room.

"'Look here, George,' I said, 'we must find out the reason of this at once. I am certain I felt something go by me as I came downstairs. Now does that staircase lead anywhere but to our rooms?'

"George considered for a moment.

"'Yes,' he replied; 'there is a door at the end of the passage which leads up into a sort of lumber room.'

"'Then we'll explore it,' I said. 'For my part I can't go to sleep until I've got to the bottom of this. Get the man to bring a lantern along.'

"The butler looked as though he didn't half like the enterprise, and, to tell the truth, no more did I. It was the uncanniest job I ever undertook. However, we started, the three of us. First of all we searched the rooms on the floor above, where George and I slept. Everything was just as we had left it. Then I pushed open the door at the end of the corridor. A crazy-looking staircase led up into darkness. We went cautiously up, I first with a candle, then George, and last of all the butler with a lantern. At the top we stepped into a big, rather low room, with beams across the ceiling, and a rough, uneven floor. Our lights threw strange shadows into the corners, and more than once I started at what looked like a crouching human figure. We searched every corner. There was nothing to be seen but a few old boxes, a roll or two of matting, and some broken chairs. But in the far corner George pointed out to me a rickety ladder which ended at a closed trap-door. Just then I distinctly heard the curious, half groaning, half sighing sound which had already puzzled me in the corridor below. We stood still and looked at one another. We all heard the sound.

"'Whatever it is, it's up there,' I said. 'The question is, who is going up?'

"George put his candle down upon the floor and stepped upon the ladder. It cracked beneath his weight. He stopped.

"'Come down; it won't bear you,' I said. 'I shall have to go.'

"I don't know that I was ever in such a queer funk as I was while I slowly mounted that ladder, and pushed open the trap-door. I had formed no clear idea of what I expected to find there. Certainly I was not prepared for what happened. For no sooner was the trap-door fully open than there fell—literally fell—upon me from the darkness above a thing in human shape, which kicked and spat and tore at me as I stood clinging to the ladder. It lasted but a moment or so, but in that moment I lived a lifetime of terror. The ladder swayed and cracked beneath me, and I fell to the floor with the thing gripping my throat like a vise. The next instant George had stunned it with a blow from the poker and dragged it off me. It lay upon its back on the floor—a ragged, hideous, loathsome shape. And the mystery was solved."

"But you haven't told us what it really was," said one of the listeners.

The doctor smiled.

"It was the owner of the house," he replied. "He had not gone abroad. He had gone to a private lunatic asylum with homicidal mania upon him. About a fortnight before this he had managed to escape; and, having made his way to his former home, had concealed himself, with a cunning often shown by lunatics, in the loft. I suppose he had found enough to eat in his nightly rambles about the house. The only wonder is that he didn't kill someone before he was caught."

COLONEL HALIFAX'S GHOST STORY.

I HAD just come back to England, after having been some years in India, and was looking forward to meet my friends, among whom there was none I was more anxious to see than Sir Francis Lynton. We had been to Eton together, and for the short time I had been at Oxford, before entering the army, we had been at the same college. Then we had parted. He came into the title and estates of the family in Yorkshire on the death of his grandfather—his father had predeceased—and I had been over a good part of the world. One visit, indeed, I had made him in his Yorkshire home, before leaving for India, of but a few days.

It will be easily imagined how pleasant it was, two or three days after my arrival in London, to receive a letter from Lynton, saying that he had just seen in the papers that I had arrived, and, begging me to come down at once to Byfield, his place in Yorkshire.

"You are not to tell me," he said, "that you cannot come. In fact, you are to come on Monday. I have a couple of horses which will just suit you; the carriage shall meet you at Packham, and all you have got to do is to put yourself in the train which leaves Kings Cross at twelve o'clock."

Accordingly, on the day appointed, I started, in due time reached Packham, losing much time on a detestable branch line, and there found the dog-cart of Sir Francis awaiting me. I drove at once to Byfield.

The house I remembered. It was a low gable structure of no great size, with old-fashioned lattice windows, separated from the park, where were deer, by a charming terraced garden.

No sooner did the wheels crunch the gravel by the principal entrance, than, almost before the bell was rung, the porch-door opened, and there stood Lynton himself, whom I had not seen for so many years, hardly altered, and with all the joy of welcome beaming in his face. Taking me by both hands, he drew me into the house, got rid of my hat and wraps, looked me all over, and then, in a breath, began to say how glad he was to see me, what a real delight it was to have got me at last under his roof, and what a good time we would have together, like the old days over again.

He had sent my luggage up to my room, which was ready for me, and he bade me make haste and dress for dinner.

So saying he took me through a paneled hall, up an old oak staircase, and showed me my room, which, hurried as I was, I observed was hung with tapestry, and had a large four-post bed, with velvet curtains, opposite the window.

They had gone in to dinner when I came down, despite all the haste I made in dressing; but a place had been kept for me next Lady Lynton.

Besides my hosts, there were their two daughters, Colonel Lynton, a brother of Sir Francis, the chaplain, and some others, whom I do not remember distinctly.

After dinner there was some music in the hall, and a game of whist in the drawing-room, and after the ladies had gone upstairs, Lynton and I retired to the smoking-room, where we sat up talking the better part of the night. I think it must have been near three when I retired. Once in bed I slept so soundly that my servant's entrance the next morning failed to arouse me, and it was past nine when I awoke.

After breakfast and the disposal of the newspapers, Lynton retired to his letters, and I asked Lady Lynton if one of her daughters might show me the house. Elizabeth, the eldest, was summoned, and seemed in no way to dislike the task.

The house was, as already intimated, by no means large; it occupied three sides of a square, the entrance and one end of the stables making the fourth side. The interior was full of interest—passages, rooms, galleries, as well as hall, were paneled in dark wood and hung with pictures. I was shown everything on the ground

"Losing much time on a detestable branch line."

floor, and then on the first floor. Then my guide proposed that we should ascend a narrow, twisting staircase that led to a gallery. We did as proposed, and entered a handsome long room or passage leading to a small chamber at one end, in which my guide told me her father kept books and papers.

I asked if anyone slept in this gallery, as I noticed a bed and fireplace, and rods by means of which curtains might be drawn, enclosing one portion where were bed and fireplace, so as to convert it into a very cosy chamber.

She answered "No;" the place was not really used, except as a playroom; though, sometimes, if the house happened to be very full—in her great-grandfather's time—she had heard that it had been occupied.

By the time we had been over the house, and I had also been shown the garden and the stables, and introduced to the dogs, it was nearly one o'clock. We were to have an early luncheon, and to drive afterwards to see the ruins of one of the grand old Yorkshire abbeys.

This was a pleasant expedition, and we got back just in time for tea, after which there was some reading aloud. The evening passed much in the same way as the preceding one, except that Lynton, who had some business, did not go down into the smoking-room, and I took the opportunity of retiring early in order to write a letter for the Indian mail, something having been said as to the prospect of hunting the next day.

I had finished my letter, which was a long one, together with two or three others, and had just got into bed, when I heard a step overhead, as of someone walking along the gallery, which I now knew ran immediately above my room. It was a slow, heavy, measured tread which I could hear getting gradually louder and nearer, and then as gradually fading away, as it retreated into the distance.

I was startled for a moment, having been told that the gallery was unused; but the next instant it occurred to me that I had been told it communicated with a chamber where Sir Francis kept books and papers. I knew he had some writing to do, and I thought no more on the matter.

I was down the next morning at breakfast in good time. "How late you were last night," I said to Lynton, in the middle of breakfast. "I heard you overhead after one o'clock."

Lynton replied rather shortly: "Indeed you did not, for I was in bed last night before twelve."

"There was someone certainly moving overhead last night," I answered, "for I heard his steps as distinctly as I ever heard anything in my life going down the gallery."

Upon which Colonel Lynton remarked that he had often fancied he had heard steps on the staircase, when he knew that no one was about. He was apparently disposed to say more, when his brother interrupted him somewhat curtly, as I fancied, and asked me if I should feel inclined after breakfast to have a horse and go out and look for the hounds. They met a considerable way off, but if they did not find in the coverts they would first draw, a thing not improbable, they would come our way, and we might fall in with them about one o'clock and have a run. I said there was nothing I should like better. Lynton mounted me on a very nice chestnut, and the rest of the party having gone out shooting, and the young ladies being otherwise engaged, he and I started about eleven o'clock for our ride.

It was a beautiful day, soft, with a bright sun, one of those beautiful days which so frequently occur in the early part of November.

On reaching the hilltop where Lynton had expected to meet the hounds, no trace of them was to be discovered. They must have found at once, and run in a different direction. At three o'clock, after we had eaten our sandwiches, Lynton reluctantly abandoned all hopes of falling in with the hounds, and said we would return home by a slightly different route.

We had not descended the hill before we came on an old chalk quarry and the remains of a disused kiln.

I recollected the spot at once. I had been here with Sir Francis on my former visit, many years ago. "Why, bless me!" said I; "do you remember, Lynton, what happened here when I was with you before? There had been men engaged removing chalk, and they came on a skeleton under some depth of rubble. We went together to see it removed, and you said you would have it preserved till it could be examined by some ethnologist or anthropologist, any one of those dry-as-dusts, to decide whether the remains were dolichocephalous or brachycephalous—whether British, Danish, or—modern. What was the result?"

Sir Francis hesitated a moment, and then answered, "It is true, I had the remains removed."

"Was there an inquest?"

"No. I had been opening some of the tumuli on the Wolds. I had sent a crouched skeleton and some skulls to the Scarsborough museum. This, I was doubtful about—whether it was a prehistoric interment—in fact, to what date it belonged. No one thought of an inquest."

On reaching the house, one of the grooms who took the horses, in answer to a question from Lynton, said that Colonel and Mrs. Hampshire had arrived about an hour ago, and that, one of the horses being lame, the carriage in which they had driven over from Castle Frampton was to put up for the night. In the drawing-room we found Lady Lynton pouring out tea for her husband's sister and her husband, who, as we came in, exclaimed: "We have come to beg a night's lodging."

It appeared that they had been on a visit in the neighborhood, and had been obliged to leave at a moment's notice in consequence of a sudden death in the house where they were staying, and that, in the impossibility of getting a fly, their hosts had sent them over to Byfield.

"We thought," Mrs. Hampshire went on to say, "that as we were coming here the end of next week, you would not mind having us a little sooner; or that, if the house were quite full, you would be willing to put us up anywhere till Monday, and let us come back later."

Lady Lynton interposed with the remark that it was all settled; and then, turning to her husband, added: "But I want to speak to you for a moment."

They both left the room together.

Lynton came back almost immediately, and, making an excuse to show me, on a map in the hall, the point to which we had ridden, said, as soon as we were alone, with a look of considerable annoyance: "I am afraid we must ask you to change your room. Shall you mind very much? I think we can make you quite comfortable upstairs in the gallery, which is the only room available. Lady Lynton has had a good fire lit; the place is really not cold, and it will be only for a night or two. Your servant has been told to put your things together, but Lady Lynton did not like to give orders to have them actually moved before my speaking to you."

I assured him that I did not mind in the very least; that I should be quite as comfortable upstairs; but that I did mind very much their making such a fuss about a matter of that sort with an old friend like myself.

Certainly nothing could look more comfortable than my new lodging when I went upstairs to dress. There was a bright fire in the large grate, an armchair had been drawn up beside it, and all my books and writing things had been put in, with a reading-lamp in the central position, and the heavy tapestry curtains were drawn, converting this part of the gallery into a room to itself. Indeed, I felt somewhat inclined to congratulate myself on the change. The spiral staircase had been one reason against this place having been given to the Hampshires. No lady's long dress trunk could have mounted it.

Sir Francis was necessarily a good deal occupied in the evening with his sister and her husband, whom he had not seen for some time. Colonel Hampshire had also just heard that he was likely to be ordered to Egypt, and when Lynton and he retired to the smoking-room, instead of going there I went upstairs to my own room to finish a book in which I was interested. I did not, however, sit up long, and very soon went to bed.

Before doing so, I drew back the curtains on the rods, partly because I like plenty of air where I sleep, and partly also because I thought I might like to see the play of the moonlight on the floor in the portion of the gallery beyond where I lay, and where the blinds had not been drawn.

I must have been asleep for some time, for the fire, which I had left in full blaze, was gone to a few sparks wandering among the ashes, when I suddenly awoke with the impression of having heard a latch click at the further extremity of the gallery, where was the chamber containing books and papers.

I had always been a light sleeper, but on the present occasion I woke at once to complete and acute consciousness, and with a sense of stretched attention which seemed to intensify all my faculties. The wind had risen, and was blowing in fitful gusts round the house.

A minute or two passed, and I began almost to fancy I must have been mistaken, when I distinctly heard the creak of the door, and then the click of the latch falling back into place. Then I heard a sound on the boards as of one moving in the gallery. I sat up to listen, and as I did so I distinctly heard steps coming down the gallery.

"Who are you?"

I heard them approach and pass my bed; I could see nothing, all was dark; but I heard the tread proceeding toward where were the uncurtained and unshuttered windows, two in number; but the moon shone through only one of these, the nearest—the other was dark, shadowed by the chapel or some other building at right angles. The tread seemed to me to pause now and again, and then continue as before.

I now fixed my eyes intently on the one illumined window, and it appeared to me as if some dark body passed across it; but what? I listened intently, and heard the step proceed to the end of the gallery, and then return.

I again watched the lighted window, and immediately that the sound reached that portion of the long passage it ceased momentarily, and I saw, as distinctly as I ever saw anything in my life, by moonlight, a figure of a man with marked features, in what appeared to be a fur cap drawn over the brows.

It stood in the embrasure of the window, and the outline of the face was in silhouette; then it moved on, and as it moved I again heard the tread.

I was as certain as I could be that the thing, whatever it was, or the person, whoever he was, was approaching my bed.

I threw myself back in the bed, and as I did see a mass of charred wood on the hearth fell down and sent up a flash of—I fancy sparks, that gave out a glare into the darkness, and by that—red as blood—I saw a face near me.

With a cry, over which I had as little control as the scream uttered by a sleeper in the agony of a nightmare, I called, "Who are you?"

There was an instant during which my hair bristled on my head, as in the horror of the darkness I prepared to grapple with the being at my side; when a board creaked as if someone had moved, and I heard the footsteps retreat, and again the click of the latch.

The next instant there was a rush on the stairs and Lynton burst into the room, just as he had sprung out of bed, crying: "For God's sake, what is the matter? Are you ill?"

I could not answer. Lynton struck a light and leaned over the bed. Then I seized him by the arm, and said, without moving: "There has been something in this room—gone in thither."

The words were hardly out of my mouth when Lynton, following the direction of my eyes, had sprung to the end of the corridor and thrown open the door there.

He went into the room beyond, looked round it, returned, and said: "You must have been dreaming."

By this time I was out of bed.

"Look for yourself," said he, and he led me into the little room. It was bare, with cupboards and boxes, a sort of lumber place. "There is nothing beyond this," said he, "no door, no staircase. It is a blind way." Then he added: "Now pull on your dressing-gown and come downstairs to my sanctum."

I followed him, and after he had spoken to Lady Lynton, who was standing with the door of her room ajar in a state of great agitation, he turned to me, and said: "No one can have been in your room. You see, my and my wife's apartments are close below, and no one could come up the spiral staircase without passing my door. You must have had a nightmare. Directly you screamed I rushed up the steps, and met no one descending; and there is no place of concealment in the lumber-room at the end of the gallery."

Then he took me into his private snuggery, blew up the fire, lighted a lamp, and said: "I shall be really grateful if you will say nothing about this. There are some in the house and neighborhood who are silly enough as it is. You stay here, and if you do not feel inclined to go to bed, read—here are books. I must go to Lady Lynton, who is a good deal frightened, and does not like to be left alone."

He then went to his bedroom.

Sleep, as far as I was concerned, was out of the question, nor do I think Sir Francis and his wife slept much, either.

I made up the fire, and after a time took up a book, and tried to read, but it was useless.

I sat absorbed in thoughts and questionings till I heard the servants stirring in the morning. I went to my own room, left the candle burning, and got into bed. I had just fallen asleep when my servant brought me a cup of tea at eight o'clock.

At breakfast Colonel Hampshire and his wife asked if anything had happened in the night, as they had been much disturbed by noises overhead, to which Lynton replied that I had not been very well, and had an attack of cramp, and that he had been upstairs to look after me. From his manner I could see that he wished me to be silent, and I said nothing accordingly.

In the afternoon, when everyone had gone out, Sir Francis took me into his snuggery, and said: "Halifax, I am very sorry about that matter last night. It is quite true, what my brother said, that steps have been heard about this house, but I never gave heed to such things, putting all noises down to rats. But after your experiences I feel that it is due to you to tell you something, and also to make to you an explanation. There is—there was—no one in the room at the end of the corridor, except the skeleton that was discovered in the chalk-pit when you were here many years ago. I confess I had not paid much heed to it. My archæological fancies passed; I had no visits from anthropologists; the bones and skull were never shown to experts, but remain packed in a chest in that lumber-room. I confess I ought to have buried them, having no more scientific use for them, but I did not—on my word, I forgot all about them, or, at least, gave no heed to them. However, what you have gone through, and have described to me, has made me uneasy, and has also given me a suspicion that I can account for that body in a manner that had never occurred to me before."

After a pause, he added: "What I am going to tell you is known to no one else, and must not be mentioned by you—anyhow, in my lifetime. You know now that, owing to the death of my father when quite young, I and my brother and sister were brought up here with our grandfather, Sir Richard. He was an old, imperious, hot-tempered man. I will tell you what I have made out of a matter that was a mystery for long, and I will tell you afterwards how I came to unravel it. My grandfather was in the habit of going out at night with a young under-keeper, of whom he was very fond, to look after the game and see if any poachers, whom he regarded as his natural enemies, were about.

"One night, as I suppose, my grandfather had been out with the young man in question, and, returning by the plantations, where the hill is steepest, and not far from the chalk-pit you

"He and the keeper buried the body."

remarked on yesterday, they came upon a man who, though not actually belonging to the country, was well known in it as a sort of traveling tinker of indifferent character and a notorious poacher. Mind this, I am not sure it was at the place I mention; I only now surmise it. On the particular night in question, my grandfather and the keeper must have caught this man setting snares; there must have been a tussle, in the course of which, as subsequent circumstances have led me to imagine, the man showed fight, and was knocked down by one or the other of the two—my grandfather or the keeper. I believe that after having made various attempts to restore him, they found that the man was actually dead.

"They were both in great alarm and concern—my grandfather especially. He had been prominent in putting down some factory riots, and had given orders to the military to fire, whereby several lives had been lost. There was a vast outcry against him, and a certain political party had denounced him as an assassin. No man was more vituperated; yet now, in my conscience, I believe he acted with both discretion and pluck, and arrested a mischievous movement that might have led to much bloodshed. Be that as it may, my impression is that he lost his head over this fatal affair with the tinker, and that he and the keeper together buried the body secretly, not far from the place where he was killed. I now think it was in the chalk-pit, and that the skeleton found years after there belonged to this man."

"Good heavens!" I exclaimed, as at once my mind rushed back to the figure with the fur cap that I had seen against the window.

Sir Francis went on: "The sudden disappearance of the tramp, in view of his well-known habits and wandering mode of life, did not for some time excite surprise; but, later on, one or two circumstances having led to suspicion, an inquiry was set on foot, and among others, my grandfather's keepers were examined before the magistrates. It was remembered afterwards that the under-keeper in question was absent at the time of the inquiry, my grandfather having sent him with some dogs to a brother-in-law of his who lived upon the moors; but whether anyone noticed the fact, or if they did, preferred to be silent, no observations were made. Nothing came of the investigation, and the whole subject would have been dropped if it had not been that two years later, for some reasons I do not understand, but at the instigation of a magistrate recently imported into the division, whom my grandfather greatly disliked, and who was opposed to him in politics, a fresh inquiry was instituted. In the course of that inquiry it transpired that, owing to some unguarded words dropped by the under-keeper, a warrant was about to be issued for his arrest. My grandfather, who had a fit of the gout, was away from home at the time, but on hearing the news he came home at once. The evening he returned he had a long interview with the young man, who left the house after he had supped in the servants' hall. It was observed that he looked much depressed. The warrant was issued the next day, but in the meantime the keeper had disappeared. My grandfather gave orders to his people to do everything in their power to assist the authorities in the search that was at once set on foot, but was unable himself to take any share in it.

"No trace of the keeper was found, although at a subsequent period rumors circulated that he had been heard of in America. But the man having been unmarried, he gradually dropped out of remembrance, and as my grandfather never allowed the subject to be mentioned in his presence, I should probably never have known anything about it but for the vague tradition which always attaches to such events, and for this fact, that after my grandfather's death, a letter came addressed to him from somewhere in the United States from some one—the name different from that of the keeper—but alluding to the past, and implying the presence of a common secret, and, of course, with it came a request for money. I replied, mentioning the death of Sir Richard, and asking for an explanation. I did get an answer, and it is from that that I am able to fill in so much of the story. But I never learned where the man had been killed and buried, and my next letter to the fellow was returned with 'deceased' written across it. Somehow, it never occurred to me till I heard your story that possibly the skeleton in the chalk-pit might be that of the poaching tinker. I will now most assuredly have it buried in the churchyard."

"That certainly ought to be done," said I.

"And," said Sir Francis, after a pause, "I give you my word—after the burial of the bones, and you are gone, I will sleep for a week in the bed in the gallery, and report to you if I see or hear anything. If all be quiet, then—well, you form your own conclusions."

I left a day after. Before long I got a letter from my friend, brief, but to the point: "All quiet, old boy; come again."

THE GHOST OF THE COUNT.

NOT far from the Alameda, in the City of Mexico, there is a great old stone building, in which once lived a very wealthy and wicked Spanish count. The house has about four floors, and ninety rooms, more or less. The entire fourth floor is rented and occupied by a big American firm, and their bookkeeper, an American girl, has given us the following true account of the ghost that for years haunted the building. The second floor is unoccupied, as no one cares to live there for obvious reasons. And the bottom floor is also unoccupied, save for lumber rooms, empty boxes and crates and barrels. And last of all is the great patio with its tiled floor, where secretly in the night a duel was fought to the death by the wicked count and a famous Austrian prince, who was one of Maximilian's men. The count was killed.

No one knows why the duel was fought; some say it was because of a beautiful Spanish woman; some say that it was because of treasure that the two jointly "conveyed," and which the count refused to divide with his princely "socio," and more people—Mexicans—shrug their shoulders if you ask about it, and say, "Quien sabe?"

"I saw a ghost here last night, Miss James," announces our cashier with much eclat and evident pride.

So great is the shock that I gasp, and my pen drops, spattering red ink on my nice fresh cuffs, and (worse luck!) on the ledger page that I had just totted up. It is ruined, and I will have to erase it, or—something! Wretched man!

"I wish to goodness it had taken you off," I cry, wrathfully, as I look at the bespattered work. "Now will you just look here and see what you have done? I wish you and your ghosts were in——"

"Gehenna?" he inquires, sweetly; "I'll fix that—it won't take half a minute. And don't look so stern, else I won't tell you about the 'espanto.' And you will be sorry if you don't hear about it—it would make such a good story." (Insinuatingly.)

"Then go ahead with it." (Ungraciously.)

"Well, last night I was waiting for West. He was to meet me here, after which it was our intention to hit the—that is, I mean we were going out together. (I nod scornfully.) And it seems that while I was patiently waiting here, in my usual sweet-tempered way, the blank idiot had his supper and then lay down to rest himself for a while. You know how delicate he is? (Another contemptuous nod.) Unfortunately he forgot the engagement, and slept on. He says he never awoke until three o'clock, and so didn't come, thinking I wouldn't be there. Meantime I also went to sleep, and might have snoozed on until three, likewise, but for the fact that the ghost woke me——"

"Well? Do go on," I urge.

"The ghost woke me, as I said," proceeds the simpleton, slowly. "It was passing its cold fingers over my face and groaning. Really, it was most extraordinary. At first I didn't know what it was; then, as I felt the icy fingers stroking my face and heard blood-curdling groans issuing from the darkness, I knew what it was. And I remembered the story of the prince and his little duel down in the patio, and knew it was the ghost of the prince's victim. By the way, you don't know what a funny sensation it is to have a ghost pat your face, Miss James——"

"Pat nothing," I retort, indignantly. "I wonder you are not ashamed to tell me such fibs. Such a ta-ra-diddle! And as for the man that the prince killed downstairs, you know as well as I do that he was taken home to Spain and buried there. Why, then, should he come back here, into our offices, and pat your face?"

"Ah, that I can't say," with a supercilious drawl. "I can only account for it by thinking that the ghost has good taste—better than that of some people I know," meaningly. "But honestly, I swear that I am telling you the truth—cross my heart and hope to die if I am not! And you don't know how brave I was—I never screamed; in fact, I never made a sound; oh, I was brave!"

"Then what did you do?" sternly.

"I ran. Por Dios, how I ran! You remember with what alacrity we got down the stairs during the November earthquake? (I remember only too distinctly.) Well, last night's run wasn't a run, in comparison—it was a disappearance, a flight, a sprint! I went down the four flights of stairs like a streak of blue lightning, and the ghost flew with me. I heard the pattering of its steps and its groans clean down to the patio door, and I assure you I quite thought I had made such an impression that it was actually going on home with me. And the thought made me feel so weak that I felt perforce obliged to take a—have a—that is, strengthen myself with a cocktail. After which I felt stronger and went home quite peacefully. But it was an uncanny experience, wasn't it?"

"Was it before or after taking that cocktail?" I ask, incredulously. "And did you take one only or eleven?"

I am hard on the man, but he really deserves it. Ghosts! Spirits, perhaps, but not ghosts. Whereat his feelings are quite "hurted"—so much so that he vows he will never tell me anything again; I had better read about Doubting Thomas; he never has seen such an unbelieving woman in all his life, and if I were only a man he would be tempted to pray that I might see the ghost; it would serve me right. Then, wrathfully departs, to notice me no more that day.

Not believing the least bit in ghosts I gave the matter no more thought. In fact, when you fall heir to a set of books that haven't been posted for nineteen days, and you have to do it all, and get up your trial balance, too, or else give up your Christmas holidays, you haven't much time to think about ghosts, or anything else, except entries. And though I had been working fourteen hours per day, the 24th of December, noon hour, found me with a difference of $13.89. The which I, of course, must locate and straighten out before departing next morning on my week's holiday. Por supuesto, it meant night work. Nothing else would do; and besides, our plans had all been made to leave on the eight o'clock train next morning. So I would just sit up all night, if need be, and find the wretched balance and be done with it.

Behold me settled for work that night at seven o'clock in my own office, with three lamps burning to keep it from looking dismal and lonely, and books and ledgers and journals piled up two feet high around me. If hard work would locate that nasty, hateful $13.89 it would surely be found. I had told the portero downstairs on the ground floor to try and keep awake for a time, but if I didn't soon finish the work I would come down and call him when I was ready to go home.

He lived in a little room, all shut off from the rest of the building, so that it was rather difficult to get at him. Besides, he was the very laziest and sleepiest peon possible, and though he was supposed to take care of the big building at night, patrolling it so as to keep off ladrones, he in reality slept so soundly that the last trumpet, much less Mexican robbers, would not have roused him.

And for this very reason, before settling to my work I was careful to go around and look to locks and bolts myself; everything was secure, and the doors safely fastened. So that if ladrones did break through they would have to be in shape to pass through keyholes or possess false keys.

With never a thought of spirits or porteros, or anything else, beyond the thirteen dollars and eighty-nine cents, I worked and added and re-added and footed up. And at eleven o'clock, grazia a Dios, I had the thirteen dollars all safe, and would have whooped for joy, had I the time. However, I wasn't out of the woods yet, the sum of eighty-nine dollars being often more easy of location than eighty-nine cents. The latter must be found, also, before I could have the pleasure of shouting in celebration thereof.

At it I went again. After brain cudgeling and more adding and prayerful thought I at last had under my thumb that abominable eighty cents. Eureka! Only nine cents out. I could get it all straight and have some sleep, after all! Inspired by which thought I smothered my yawns and again began to add. I looked at my watch—ten minutes to twelve. Perhaps I could get it fixed before one.

I suppose I had worked at the nine cents for about twenty minutes. One of the cash entries looked to me to be in error. I compared it with the voucher—yes, that was just where the trouble lay! Eleven cents—ten—nine——

S-t-t! Out went the lights in the twinkling of an eye—as I sat, gaping in my astonishment, from out of the pitchy darkness of the room came the most dreary, horrible, blood-curdling groan imaginable. As I sat paralyzed, not daring to breathe, doubting my senses for a moment, and then thinking indignantly that it was some trick of that wretched cashier, I felt long, thin, icy fingers passing gently over my face. Malgame Dios! what a sensation! At first I was afraid to move. Then I nervously tried to brush the icy, bony things away. As fast as I brushed, with my heart beating like a steam-hammer, and gasping with deadly fear, the fingers would come back again; a cold wind was blowing over me. Again came that dreadful groan, and too frightened to move or scream, I tumbled in a heap on the floor, among the books and ledgers. Then I suppose I fainted.

When I regained my senses I was still in a heap with the ledgers; still it was dark and still I felt the cold fingers caressing my face. At which I became thoroughly desperate. No ghost should own me! I had laughed at the poor cashier and hinted darkly at cocktails. Pray, what better was I?

I scrambled to my feet, the fingers still stroking my face. I must address them—what language—did they understand English or Spanish, I wondered? Spanish would doubtless be most suitable, if indeed, it was the ghost of the murdered count——.

"Will you do me the favor, Senor Ghost," I started out bravely, in my best Spanish, but with a very trembling voice, "to inform me what it is that you desire? Is there anything I can do for you? Because, if not, I would like very much to be allowed to finish my work, which I cannot do (if you will pardon my abruptness) if I am not alone."

(Being the ghost of a gentleman and a diplomat, surely he would take the hint and vanish. Ojala!)

Perhaps the ghost did not understand my Spanish; at any rate there was no articulate reply; there was another groan—again the fingers touched me, and then there was such a mournful sigh that I felt sorry for the poor thing—what could be the matter with it? With my pity, all fear was lost for a moment, and I said to the darkness all about me:

"What is it that you wish, pobre senor? Can I not aid you? I am not afraid—let me help you!"

The fingers moved uncertainly for a moment; then the ledgers all fell down, with a loud bang; a cold hand caught mine, very gently—I tried not to feel frightened, but it was difficult—and I was led off blindly, through the offices. I could not see a thing—not a glimmer of light showed; not a sound was heard except my own footsteps, and the faint sound of the invisible something that was leading me along—there were no more groans, thank goodness, else I should have shrieked and fainted, without a doubt. Only the pattering footsteps and the cold hand that led me on and on.

We—the fingers and I—were somehow in the great hall, then on the second floor, and at last on the stairs, going on down, flight after flight. Then I knew that I was being led about by the fingers on the tiled floor of the patio, and close to the portero's lodge. Simpleton that he was! Sleeping like a log, no doubt, while I was being led about in the black darkness by an invisible hand, and no one to save me! I would have yelled, of course, but for one fact—I found it utterly impossible to speak or move my tongue, being a rare and uncomfortable sensation.

But where were we going? Back into the unused lumber rooms, joining onto the patio? Nothing there, except barrels and slabs and empty boxes. What could the ghost mean? He must be utterly demented, surely.

In the middle of the first room we paused. I had an idea of rushing out and screaming for the portero, but abandoned it when I found that my feet wouldn't go. I heard steps passing to and fro about the floor, and waited, cold and trembling. They approached me; again my hand was taken, and I was led over near the corner of the room. Obedient to the unseen will, I bent down and groped about the floor, guided by the cold fingers holding mine, until I felt something like a tiny ring, set firmly in the floor. I pulled at it faintly, but it did not move, at which the ghost gave a faint sigh. For a second the cold fingers pressed mine, quite affectionately, then released me, and I heard steps passing slowly into the patio, then dying away. Where was it going, and what on earth did it all mean?

But I was so tired and wrought up I tried to find the door, but couldn't (the cashier would have been revenged could he have seen me stupidly fumbling at a barrel, thinking it was the door), and at last, too fatigued and sleepy to stand, I dropped down on the cold stone floor and went to sleep.

I must have slept for some hours, for when I awoke the light of dawn was coming in at the window, and I sat up and wondered if I had taken leave of my senses during the night. What on earth could I be doing here in the lumber-room? Then, like a flash, I remembered, and, half unconsciously, crept about on the floor seeking the small ring. There it was! I caught it and jerked at it hard. Hey, presto, change! For it seemed to me that the entire floor was giving way. There was a sliding, crashing sound, and I found myself hanging on for dear life to a barrel that, fortunately, retained its equilibrium, and with my feet dangling into space. Down below me was a small, stone-floored room, with big boxes and small ones ranged about the walls. Treasure! Like a flash the thought struck me, and with one leap I was down in the secret room gazing about at the boxes.

But, alas! upon investigation, the biggest chests proved empty. The bad, wicked count! No wonder he couldn't rest in his Spanish grave, but must come back to the scene of his wickedness and deceit to make reparation! But the smaller chests were literally crammed with all sorts of things—big heavy Spanish coins, in gold and silver—gold and silver dinner services, with the crest of the unfortunate emperor; magnificent pieces of jeweled armor and weapons, beautiful jewelry and loose precious stones. I deliberately selected handfuls of the latter, giving my preference to the diamonds and pearls—I had always had a taste for them, which I had never before been able to gratify!—and packed them in a wooden box that I found in the lumber-room. The gold and dinner services and armor, etc., I left as they were, being rather cumbersome, and carried off, rejoicing, my big box of diamonds and pearls and other jewelry.

Needless to say we didn't go away for the holidays on the eight o'clock train. But I did come down to the office and proceeded to locate my missing nine cents. After which I unfolded the tale of the ghost and the treasure—only keeping quiet the matter of my private loot. Of which I was heartily glad afterwards. For when the government learned of the find what do you suppose they offered me for going about with the ghost and discovering the secret room and treasure? Ten thousand dollars! When I refused, stating that I would take merely, as my reward, one of the gold dinner services, the greedy things objected at first, but I finally had my way. And to this very day they have no idea that I—even I—have all the beautiful jewels. Wouldn't they be furious if they knew it? But they aren't apt to, unless they learn English and read this story. Which isn't likely.

THE OLD MANSION.

DOWN on Long Beach, that narrow strip of sand which stretches along the New Jersey coast from Barnegat Inlet on the north to Little Egg Harbor Inlet on the south, the summer sojourner at some one of the numerous resorts, which of late years have sprung up every few miles, may, in wandering over the sand dunes just across the bay from the village of Manahawkin, stumble over some charred timbers or vestiges of crumbling chimneys, showing that once, years back, a human habitation has stood there. If the find rouses the jaded curiosity of the visitor sufficiently to impel him to question the weatherbeaten old bayman who sails him on his fishing trips he will learn that these relics mark the site of one of the first summer hotels erected on the New Jersey coast.

"That's where the Old Mansion stood," he will be informed by Captain Nate or Captain Sam, or whatever particular captain it may chance to be, and if by good fortune it chances to be Captain Jim, he will hear a story that will pleasantly pass away the long wait for a sheepshead bite.

It was my good luck to have secured Captain Jim for a preceptor in the angler's art during my vacation last summer, and his stories and reminiscences of Long Beach were not the least enjoyable features of the two weeks' sojourn.

Captain Jim was not garrulous. Few of the baymen are. They are a sturdy, self-reliant and self-controlled people, full of strong common sense, but still with that firm belief in the supernatural which seems inherent in dwellers by the sea.

"The Old Mansion," said Captain Jim, "or the Mansion of Health, for that was its full name, was built away back in 1822, so I've heard my father say. There had been a tavern close by years before that was kept by a man named Cranmer, and people used to come from Philadelphia by stage, sixty miles through the pines, to 'Hawkin, and then cross here by boat. Some would stop at Cranmer's and others went on down the beach to Homer's which was clear down at End by the Inlet. Finally some of the wealthy people concluded that they wanted better accommodations than Cranmer gave, so they formed the Great Swamp Long Beach Company, and built the Mansion of Health. I've heard that when it was built it was the biggest hotel on the coast, and was considered a wonder. It was 120 feet long, three stories high, and had a porch running all the way around it, with a balcony on top. It was certainly a big thing for those days. I've heard father tell many a time of the stage loads of gay people that used to come rattling into 'Hawkin, each stage drawn by four horses, and sometimes four or five of them a day in the summer. A good many people, too, used to come in their own carriages, and leave them over on the mainland until they were ready to go home. There were gay times at the Old Mansion then, and it made times good for the people along shore, too."

"How long did the Old Mansion flourish, Captain?" I asked.

"Well, for twenty-five or thirty years people came there summer after summer. Then they built a railroad to Cape May, and that, with the ghosts, settled the Mansion of Health."

"What do you mean by the ghosts?" I demanded.

"Well, you see," said Captain Jim, cutting off a mouthful of navy plug, "the story got around that the old house was haunted. Some people said there were queer things seen there, and strange noises were heard that nobody could account for, and pretty soon the place got a bad name and visitors were so few that it didn't pay to keep it open any more."

"But how did it get the name of being haunted, Captain Jim?" I persisted.

"Why, it was this way," continued the mariner. "Maybe you've heard of the time early in the fifties when the Powhatan was wrecked on the beach here, and every soul on board was lost. She was an emigrant ship, and there were over 400 people aboard—passengers and crew. She came ashore here during the equinoctial storm in September. There wasn't any life-saving stations in them days, and everyone was drowned. You can see the long graves now over in the 'Hawkin churchyard, where the bodies were buried after they came ashore. They put them in three long trenches that were dug from one end of the burying-ground to the other. The only people on the beach that night was the man who took care of the old mansion. He lived there with his family, and his son-in-law lived with him. He was the wreckmaster for this part of the coast, too. It wasn't till the second day that the people from 'Hawkin could get over to the beach, and by that time the bodies had all come ashore, and the wreckmaster had them all piled up on the sand. I was a youngster, then, and came over with my father, and, I tell you, it was the awfullest sight I ever saw—them long rows of drowned people, all lying there with their white, still faces turned up to the sky. Some were women, with their dead babies clasped tight in their arms, and some were husbands and wives, whose bodies came ashore locked together in a death embrace. I'll never forget that sight as long as I live. Well, when the coroner came and took charge he began to inquire whether any money or valuables had been found, but the wreckmaster declared that not a solitary coin had been washed ashore. People thought this was rather singular, as the emigrants were, most of them, well-to-do Germans, and were known to have brought a good deal of money with them, but it was concluded that it had gone down with the ship. Well, the poor emigrants were given pauper burial, and the people had begun to forget their suspicions until three or four months later there came another storm, and the sea broke clear over the beach, just below the Old Mansion, and washed away the sand. Next morning early two men from 'Hawkin sailed across the bay and landed on the beach. They walked across on the hard bottom where the sea had washed across, and, when about half way from the bay, one of the men saw something curious close up against the stump of an old cedar tree. He called the other man's attention to it, and they went over to the stump. What they found was a pile of leather money-belts that would have filled a wheelbarrow. Every one was cut open and empty. They had been buried in the sand close by the old stump, and the sea had washed away the covering. The men didn't go any further.

"They carried the belts to their boats and sailed back to 'Hawkin as fast as the wind would take them. Of course, it made a big sensation, and everybody was satisfied that the wreckmaster had robbed the bodies, if he hadn't done anything worse, but there was no way to prove it, and so nothing was done. The wreckmaster didn't stay around here long after that, though. The people made it too hot for him, and he and his family went away South, where it was said he bought a big plantation and a lot of slaves. Years afterward the story came to 'Hawkin somehow that he was killed in a barroom brawl, and that his son-in-law was drowned by his boat upsettin' while he was out fishin'. I don't furnish any affidavits with that part of the story, though.

"However, after that nobody lived in the Old Mansion for long at a time. People would go there, stay a week or two, and leave—and at last it was given up entirely to beach parties in the day time, and ghosts at night."

"But, Captain, you don't really believe the ghost part, do you?" I asked.

Captain Jim looked down the bay, expectorated gravely over the side of the boat, and answered, slowly:

"Well, I don't know as I would have believed in 'em if I hadn't seen the ghost."

"What!" I exclaimed; "you saw it? Tell me about it. I've always wanted to see a ghost, or next best thing, a man who has seen one."

"It was one August, about 1861," said the captain. "I was a young feller then, and with a half dozen more was over on the beach cutting salt hay. We didn't go home at nights, but did our own cooking in the Old Mansion kitchen, and at nights slept on piles of hay upstairs. We were a reckless lot of scamps, and reckoned that no ghosts could scare us. There was a big full moon that night, and it was as light as day. The musketeers was pretty bad, too, and it was easier to stay awake than go to sleep. Along toward midnight me and two other fellers went out on the old balcony, and began to race around the house. We hollered and yelled, and chased each other for half an hour or so, and then we concluded we had better go to sleep, so we started for the window of the room where the rest were. This window was near one end on the ocean side, and as I came around the corner I stopped as if I had been shot, and my hair raised straight up on top of my head. Right there in front of that window stood a woman looking out over the sea, and in her arms she held a little child. I saw her as plain as I see you now. It seemed to me like an hour she stood there, but I don't suppose it was a second; then she was gone. When I could move I looked around for the other boys, and they were standing there paralyzed. They had seen the woman, too. We didn't say much, and we didn't sleep much that night, and the next night we bunked out on the beach. The rest of the crowd made all manner of fun of us, but we had had all the ghost we wanted, and I never set foot inside the old house after that."

"When did it burn down, Captain?" I asked, as Jim relapsed into silence.

"Somewhere about twenty-five years ago. A beach party had been roasting clams in the old oven, and in some way the fire got to the woodwork. It was as dry as tinder, and I hope the ghosts were all burnt up with it."

A MISFIT GHOST.

EVERY boy with a knowledge of adventurous literature, otherwise "novels of action," knows of the "phantom ship," the spook of the high seas.

But it has not been known that ships themselves are haunted, and that in the service of the United States Coast Survey there is a vessel now in commission that is by her own officers supposed to be haunted.

Yet the Eagre, a 140-foot schooner of the coast survey, is looked upon in the service as a very undesirable vessel to be aboard of. About her there is an atmosphere of gloom that wardroom jest cannot dispel.

Duty on board her has been shunned as would be a pestilence, and stories have been told by officers who have cruised aboard her that are not good for timid people to hear. Officers have hesitated about telling these uncanny stories, but they have become sufficiently well known to make a billet to duty aboard the Eagre unwelcome among the coast survey men.

The Mohawk was launched June 10, 1875, at Greenpoint, and she was then the largest sailing yacht afloat.

William T. Garner, her young millionaire owner, was very proud of his new craft, and all the then leaders of New York society were invited to participate in the good time afloat with which her launching was celebrated. Commodore Garner, then but thirty-three years old, and his young wife entertained charmingly, and the trim, speedy Mohawk was christened with unusually merry festivities. Soon after that she was capsized by a sudden squall off the landing at Stapleton, N. Y., and six people were drowned like rats in her cabin and forecastle.

Then the Mohawk was raised at a cost of $25,000 and purchased by the United States Government for the service of the coast survey. Her name was changed to Eagre, for Jack Tar is proverbially superstitious, and with the old name it would have been impossible to ship a crew.

Lieutenant Higby King describes his initial experience when he was assigned to duty on the Eagre in this way:

"She had her full complement of officers minus one when I boarded her at Newport to complete the list. Every cabin was occupied but the port cabin by the companion way, and to that I was assigned.

"We had a jolly wardroom mess that night, and I retired from it early, as I was tired by my journey to join the vessel. The others who were still at the table regarded my retirement to the port cabin in absolute silence, having bidden me good-night. Their silence did not lead me to suspect anything, though I knew that the Eagre had once been the Mohawk. My cabin door had the usual cabin lock of brass, and the porthole was also securely fastened. There could have been no one under the bed or sofa, as beneath each was a facing of solid oak paneling.

"I undressed lazily and left the light burning dimly in my bracket lamp. I tried conscientiously to go to sleep for I don't know how long with my back turned to the light. The noise ceased in the wardroom after a time, and I knew the others had turned in, but I felt unaccountably nervous and restless. I turned over and faced the light, thoroughly wide awake, and there in the single chair sat an elderly man, seemingly wrapt in deep thought. He was dressed in a blue yachting reefer, and had a long, gray beard. His hands were clasped in his lap, and his eyes were downcast. His face was not pale and ghastly, as the faces of ghosts are popularly supposed to be, but ruddy and weatherbeaten.

"I regarded him in scared silence for I don't know how long, though it seemed an hour when he, or it, or whatever it was, disappeared. During that time the ghost, and such I now believe it to have been, made not a motion, nor did it say anything. Presently I looked again, and it was gone.

"At breakfast the others watched me critically as I took my seat. I had not intended to say anything about my experience, for I thought then I had seen some sort of hallucination and strongly suspected that I was verging on insanity. Lieutenant Irving asked me if I had slept well. I replied that I had. 'Didn't you see anything?' he inquired. I then frankly admitted that I had and described my experience. Then I learned that each one of the seven others present had tried the port cabin at one time or another, and each had seen the self-same apparition. It had acted in exactly the same way in each case, except in the case of Irving, who shot at it with his pistol, when it immediately disappeared. Some of the others had been led by their curiosity to inquire if anyone lost on the Mohawk resembled the figure, and found that none of the unfortunate ones at all fitted the description. It had been dubbed by them the 'misfit ghost.' That one experience was enough for me, and after that I, by courtesy, shared the cabin of another fellow."

Lieutenant Irving and others corroborate the story of Lieutenant King, and as additional evidence that the Eagre is haunted, Lieutenant Irving describes a New Year's eve experience of the Eagre's officers, that is, to say the least, novel in the way of supernatural manifestations.

"It was at mess. The first toast, 'Sweethearts and Wives,' had been drunk, as it always is by Yankee sailors the world over on occasions of festivity. Everyone was feeling happy, or, as Thackeray has it, 'pleasant,' when suddenly the sliding-doors separating the wardroom from the companion way closed slowly with a loud, squeaking noise. They had seldom been closed, and it took the entire strength of a man to start them from their rusty fastenings. Yet upon this occasion they started easily and closed tightly, while the officers jumped to their feet in breathless astonishment. Half a dozen men hauled them open in haste, but not a soul was behind them or anywhere about. 'It must be our old friend of the port cabin,' suggested one, and in awe-stricken silence the health of the 'misfit ghost' was drunk."

AN UNBIDDEN GUEST.

My cousins, Kate and Tom Howard, married at Trinity, at Easter time, concluded to commence housekeeping by taking one of those delightfully expensively furnished, unfurnished cottages, with which the fashionable watering place of W—— abounds, from whose rear windows one might almost take a plunge into the surf, the beach beginning at the back door. They went down quite early in May, being in a great hurry to try their domestic experiment; and, as the evenings were still cold, they spent them about the open fire, "spooning."

It was upon one of those nights, about eleven o'clock, that they were startled by a noise, as of some small object falling, soon followed by the sound of heavy footsteps, and then quiet again reigned supreme. At once Tom, poker in hand, boldly started in search of the burglar, followed by Kate, wildly clutching at his coat-tail, and in a state of tremor. They looked upstairs, under the various beds, Kate suggesting that in novels they were always to be found there.

The dining-room was next explored, where all seemed well, and, lastly the kitchen, where they found what was evidently a solution of the mystery. The burglar had entered by the back door, which was found to be unlocked and slightly ajar. The first excitement subsiding, they returned again to the dining-room, where Tom, upon closer inspection, then discovered that one of a pair of quaint little pepper-pots, wedding gifts, was missing, and other small articles on the sideboard had been slightly disturbed.

The next morning, when Kate mildly remonstrated with the queen of the kitchen for her carelessness, she received a shock by being told that it was her usual custom to leave the door open, "so that it would be aisy, convanient loike for the milkmaid." They parted with her, and a new maid was engaged, whose chief qualification for the place was that she was most faithful in the discharge of her duties, especially in "locking up."

While they mourned the loss of the pepper-pot, still it seemed so trifling when they thought of that lovely repousse salad bowl, sent by Aunt Julia, which stood near by, that nothing was said of the loss outside of the family, and the little household settled into its normal state once more of "billing and cooing."

About a fortnight later, Tom started out one night with an old fisherman, one of the natives, and a local "character," to indulge in that delightful pastime, so dear to the heart of man, known as "eeling," and, as the night was dark, the eels were particularly "sporty," so that it was well on towards the "wee sma' hours" when Tom at last returned to the cottage.

He found all excitement within. Kate was in hysterics, and the new maid, also weeping, was industriously applying the camphor bottle to her mistress' nose. The burglar, or ghost, as they had now decided, the windows and doors being found to be securely locked this time, had been abroad again, but had succeeded in purloining nothing. His royal ghostship had amused himself, apparently, by simply walking about.

"Oh, Tom! he had on such heavy boots and was so dreadfully bold about it," said Kate, tearfully.

From that time Kate became nervous and refused to be left alone. Tom started whenever a door creaked, and the "treasure" departed hurriedly, saying, "Faith, the house is haunted, sure."

After that Kate spent her days in "girl hunting," and her nights in answering shadowy advertisements that never materialized. They tried Irish, English, Dutch, and a "heathen Chinee," with a sprinkling of "colored ladies" to vary the monotony. They seemed about to become famous throughout the length and breadth of the land as "the family that changes help once a week," when they landed Treasure No. 2.

Shortly after her advent we were all asked down to W——, to help celebrate their happiness, and incidentally to christen the new dinner set. We were not a little surprised at finding Kate so pale and Tom rather distrait. However, after a delightful dinner, that should have filled with pleasure the most exacting bride, we adjourned to the piazza, leaving the men to the contemplation of their cigars. We were enthusiastic in our praise of the house, and congratulated Kate in securing such a prize, when, to our horror, she burst into tears, and said: "Oh, girls, it's a dreadful place; it's haunted!" and then tearfully proceeded with the details, until we all felt creepy and suggested the parlor and lights.

It was not until long afterwards that Kate discovered that Tom had also related the "ghost story" to the men, that evening, to which Ned Harris had said, laconically, "Rats," and Bob Shaw laughingly remarked, "Tom, old chap, you really shouldn't take your nightcap so strong."

About the first of July the climax came. The ghost walked again, this time taking not only the remaining pepper-pot, but also a silver salt-cellar. Evidently he had a penchant for small articles, but unlike former times, everything on the sideboard was in the greatest disorder. Aunt Julia's salad bowl was found on the floor, and not far away the cheese-dish, with its contents scattered about. This time one of the windows was found half open. A week later a note came to me from Kate, saying that she and Tom had gone to Saratoga to spend the remainder of the season with her mother.

The following spring Tom received a note and parcel from Mr. B——, the owner of the house at W——, which read as follows:

DEAR MR. HOWARD: I send you by express three articles of silver, which my wife suggests may belong to you, as they are marked with your initials, namely, two silver pepper-pots and a salt-cellar; they were found, the other day, during the process of spring house cleaning, in a rat hole, behind the sideboard. I forgot to have the holes stopped up last spring, or to caution you against the water rats; the great fellows will get in, you know. Kind regards to Mrs. Howard.

Very truly,

JOHN B——.

The next season the "Ghost Club" was organized, the badge being a small silver rat, bearing proudly aloft a tiny pepper-pot. We thoughtfully offered Tom the presidency, but he declined, with offended dignity, from the effects of which I think he will never fully recover.

THE DEAD WOMAN'S PHOTOGRAPH.

VIRGIL HOYT is a photographer's assistant up at St. Paul, and a man of a good deal of taste. He has been in search of the picturesque all over the West, and hundreds of miles to the north in Canada, and can speak three or four Indian dialects, and put a canoe through the rapids. That is to say, he is a man of an adventurous sort and no dreamer. He can fight well and shoot well and swim well enough to put up a winning race with the Indian boys, and he can sit all day in the saddle and not dream about it at night.

Wherever he goes he uses his camera.

"The world," Hoyt is in the habit of saying to those who sit with him when he smokes his pipe, "was created in six days to be photographed. Man—and especially woman—was made for the same purpose. Clouds are not made to give moisture, nor trees to cast shade. They were created for the photographer."

In short, Virgil Hoyt's view of the world is whimsical, and he doesn't like to be bothered with anything disagreeable. That is the reason that he loathes and detests going to a house of mourning to photograph a corpse. The horribly bad taste of it offends him partly, and partly he is annoyed at having to shoulder, even for a few moments, a part of someone's burden of sorrow. He doesn't like sorrow, and would willingly canoe 500 miles up the cold Canadian rivers to get rid of it. Nevertheless, as assistant photographer, it is often his duty to do this very kind of thing.

Not long ago he was sent for by a rich Jewish family at St. Paul to photograph the mother, who had just died. He was very much put out, but he went. He was taken to the front parlor, where the dead woman lay in her coffin. It was evident that there was some excitement in the household and that a discussion was going on, but Hoyt wasn't concerned, and so he paid no attention to the matter.

The daughter wanted the coffin turned on end, in order that the corpse might face the camera properly, but Hoyt said he could overcome the recumbent attitude and make it appear that the face was taken in the position it would naturally hold in life, and so they went out and left him alone with the dead.

The face was a strong and positive one, such as may often be seen among Jewish matrons. Hoyt regarded it with some admiration, thinking to himself that she was a woman who had been used to having her own way. There was a strand of hair out of place, and he pushed it back from her brow. A bud lifted its head too high from among the roses on her breast and spoiled the contour of the chin, so he broke it off. He remembered these things later very distinctly and that his hand touched her bare face two or three times.

Then he took the photographs and left the house.

He was very busy at the time and several days elapsed before he was able to develop the plates. He took them from the bath, in which they had lain with a number of others, and went to work upon them. There were three plates, he having taken that number merely as a precaution against any accident. They came up well, but as they developed he became aware of the existence of something in the photograph which had not been apparent to his eye. The mysterious always came under the head of the disagreeable with him, and was therefore to be banished, so he made only a few prints and put the things away out of sight. He hoped that something would intervene to save him from attempting an explanation.

But it is a part of the general perplexity of life that things do not intervene as they ought and when they ought, so one day his employer asked him what had become of those photographs. He

"They left him alone with the dead."

tried to evade him, but it was futile, and he got out the finished photographs and showed them to him. The older man sat staring at them a long time.

"Hoyt," said he, at length, "you're a young man, and I suppose you have never seen anything like this before. But I have. Not exactly the same thing, but similar phenomena have come my way a number of times since I went into the business, and I want to tell you there are things in heaven and earth not dreamt of——"

"Oh, I know all that tommy-rot," cried Hoyt, angrily, "but when anything happens I want to know the reason why, and how it is done."

"All right," said his employer, "then you might explain why and how the sun rises."

But he humored the younger man sufficiently to examine with him the bath in which the plates were submerged and the plates themselves. All was as it should be. But the mystery was there and could not be done away with.

Hoyt hoped against hope that the friends of the dead woman would somehow forget about the photographs, but of course the wish was unreasonable, and one day the daughter appeared and asked to see the photographs of her mother.

"Well, to tell the truth," stammered Hoyt, "those didn't come out as well as we could wish."

"But let me see them," persisted the lady. "I'd like to look at them, anyway."

"He showed her the prints."

"Well, now," said Hoyt, trying to be soothing, as he believed it was always best to be with women—to tell the truth, he was an ignoramus where women were concerned—"I think it would be better if you didn't see them. There are reasons why——" he ambled on like this, stupid man that he was, and of course the Jewess said she would see those pictures without any further delay.

So poor Hoyt brought them out and placed them in her hand, and then ran for the water pitcher, and had to be at the bother of bathing her forehead to keep her from fainting.

For what the lady saw was this: Over face and flowers and the head of the coffin fell a thick veil, the edges of which touched the floor in some places. It covered the features so well that not a hint of them was visible.

"There was nothing over mother's face," cried the lady at length.

"Not a thing," acquiesced Hoyt. "I know, because I had occasion to touch her face just before I took the picture. I put some of her hair back from her brow."

"What does it mean, then?" asked the lady.

"You know better than I. There is no explanation in science. Perhaps there is some in psychology."

"Well," said the lady, stammering a little and coloring, "mother was a good woman, but she always wanted her own way, and she always had it, too."

"Yes?"

"And she never would have her picture taken. She didn't admire herself. She said no one should ever see a picture of hers."

"So?" said Hoyt, meditatively. "Well, she's kept her word, hasn't she?"

The two stood looking at the pictures for a time. Then Hoyt pointed to the open blaze in the grate.

"Throw them in," he commanded. "Don't let your father see them—don't keep them yourself. They wouldn't be good things to keep."

"That's true enough," said the lady, slowly. And she threw them in the fire. Then Virgil Hoyt brought out the plates and broke them before her eyes.

And that was the end of it—except that Hoyt sometimes tells the story to those who sit beside him when his pipe is lighted.

THE GHOST OF A LIVE MAN.

WE were in the South Atlantic Ocean, in the latitude of the island of Fernando Norohna, about 40 degrees 12 minutes south, on board the barque H. G. Johnson, homeward bound from Australia. I was the only passenger, and we had safely rounded Cape Horn, with the barometer at 28 degrees 18 minutes, and yet had somehow miraculously escaped any extremely heavy gale—had had light northerly and easterly winds till we reached 20 degrees, and thence the southeast trades were sending us fast on our way to the equator. I sat on deck smoking my pipe, with a glorious full moon shedding its bright pathway across the blue waters, and chatting with the first mate, a man some fifty-eight years of age, who had followed the sea since he was a boy. For twenty years or more he had been mate or captain, and many and varied were the experiences he could relate. A thorough sailor and skillful navigator, he was as honest as the day is long—had a heart as big as an ox and was an all-round good fellow and genial companion. Some of his yarns might be taken cum grano salis, yet he always positively assured me that he "was telling me the truth." An account of a voyage that he made in a whaler from the Southern Ocean to New Bedford seemed to me worthy to be repeated. He had rounded Cape Horn six times and the Cape of Good Hope twenty-six times, besides making many trips across the Western Ocean and to South American ports. I give his account as near as possible in his own words:

"It was in '71 that I commanded the whaler Mary Jane. We had been out from home over three years, and had on board a full cargo of whale oil, besides 2,000 pounds of whalebone, which was then worth $5 per pound. I also had been fortunate enough to find in a dead whale which we came across a large quantity of ambergris, and our hearts were all very light as we began our homeward voyage, and our thoughts all tended to the hearty welcome which we should receive from wives and sweethearts when we reached our journey's end. Many a night as I lay in my berth I had thought with great pleasure of the amount of money that would be coming to me from the proceeds of our voyage when we arrived in New Bedford.

"I calculated that I had made $12,000 as my share of the proceeds of the whalebone and oil—to say nothing of the ambergris, which I well knew would bring at least $20,000, and one-half of which belonged to me. You can therefore imagine that I was well pleased with myself as we went bounding along through the southeast trades. We crossed the equator in longitude 36 and soon after took strong northeast trades, and all was going as well as I could wish. We had put the ship in perfect order, painted her inside and out, and you would never have recognized her as the old whaling ship that had for three years been plying the Southern Ocean for whales. Never shall I forget an old bull whale that we tackled about two degrees to the south of Cape Horn—but that is another story, which I will give you another time.

"We had just lost the northeast trades and were entering the Gulf Stream. I sat in my cabin with my chart on the table before me rolled up. I had just picked our location on it, and was thinking that in a week more I should be at home, surrounded by those near and dear to me, and relating to them the story of my great good fortune.

"It was always my custom to work up my latitude and longitude about four o'clock in the afternoon, and then after supper pick off her position on the chart, have a smoke and perhaps just before retiring a nip of grog, and then at 8.30 o'clock, as regular as a clock, I would turn in.

"I am a great smoker, and this day I had been smoking all the afternoon, besides having had two or three nips. We had a dog on board whom we called 'Bosun,' who had been out with us all the voyage, and who was afraid of nothing. He had endeared himself to every man on board, and when Bosun 'took water' something very serious was in the wind. This night as I sat in the cabin I heard a most dismal howl from Bosun, and called out to the mate to know what was the matter with the dog. He replied that he 'reckoned some of the men had been teasing him,' and the occurrence soon passed from my mind.

"Suddenly I saw someone coming down the after companion way into the cabin. I supposed at first it was the mate and wondered that he had not first spoken to me, but then I noticed that he wore clothes I had never seen on the mate, and as he advanced into the cabin I saw his face. It was the face of a man I had never seen in my life. He was thin and pale and haggard, and as he advanced he looked about the cabin and at the rolled up chart on the table. There seemed to be an appeal in his eyes, and then there swept over his face a look of intense disappointment, and before I could move or speak, he had vanished from my sight.

"Now I am a very practical man, and I at once straightened myself in my chair and said to myself: 'Well, old man, you have smoked one too many pipes to-day, or else you have had one drink too much, for you have been asleep in your chair and seen a ghost.' I was quite satisfied that I had had a dream, especially as I called to the mate and asked him if he had seen anyone come below. He said no; that he had not left the deck for the last hour, and the man at the wheel, directly in front of the door, was sure no one had entered the cabin, so I convinced myself that I had had a very vivid dream— though I could not help thinking of the matter all through the next day.

"At eight o'clock the next evening I sat in the same place with my work just finished and the chart lying rolled up on the table before me, when suddenly the dog's dismal howl rang through the ship, and looking up I saw those same legs coming down the after companion. My hair fairly stood on end, and yet to-day surely I was wide awake. I had only smoked one pipe all day, and had not touched a drop of liquor. The same wan, emaciated figure walked into the cabin, glanced inquiringly and appealingly at me, and again there spread over his face that look of utter disappointment as if he had sought something and failed to find it, and again he disappeared. I rushed on deck to the mate and told him all I had seen during the last two nights; but he made light of it, and assured me I had been asleep or smoking too much. He did not like to suggest that I had been drinking. Still, I could see that the thought that came into his mind was 'The old man has seen 'em again.' I gave up trying to convince him, but requested that the next night, from 8 to 8.30, he should sit with me in the cabin.

"How the next day passed I cannot tell. I only know that my thoughts never left that ghostly visitant, and somehow I felt that the evening would reveal something to me and the spell be broken. I made up my mind I would speak to the thing, whatever it was, and I felt a sort of security in the presence of the mate, who was a daring fellow and feared neither man nor the devil. Neither rum nor tobacco passed my lips during the next day, and eight o'clock found the mate and I sitting in the cabin, and this time the chart lay open on the table beside us. Just as eight bells struck the dog's premonitory wail sounded, and looking up we both saw the figure descending the cabin stairs. We both seemed frozen to our seats, and the strange weirdness of the whole proceeding cast the same spell over the mate and me alike, and we were both unable to move or speak. Slowly the figure proceeded into the cabin and glanced around without a word, but with the same expectant look on his face. His form was even more wasted, his cheeks sunken and his eyes seemed almost out of sight so deeply were they set in their sockets. As his eye fell on the open chart a look of supreme joy fairly irradiated his features, and advancing to the table he placed one long, bony finger on the chart, held it for a moment and then again disappeared from our sight.

"For five minutes after he had left us we sat speechless. Then I managed to say: 'What do you think of that, Mr. Morris?' 'My God! sir, I don't know—it's beyond me.' Then my eyes fell on the open chart and there where the finger had been was a tiny spot of blood, exactly on the point of longitude 63 degrees west and latitude 37 degrees north. We were then only about fifty miles distant from that position, and immediately there came to me the determination to steer the ship there; so I laid her course accordingly, and posted a lookout in the crow's nest. At five o'clock in the morning, just as the east began to grow gray, the lookout called out: 'Boat on the lee bow,' and as we came up to it we found four men in it—three dead and one with just a remnant of life left in him. We sewed the three bodies in canvas and buried them in the ocean, and then gave all our attention to restoring life to the poor emaciated frame, which, I then recognized, was the very man who for three successive nights had visited me in my cabin.

"By judicious and careful nursing life gradually came back to him, and in four days' time he was able to sit up and talk with me in the cabin. It seems he commanded the ship Promise, and she had taken fire and been destroyed, and all hands had to take to the boats. Ten were in the boats at first, but their food had given out, and one by one he had seen them die, and one by one he had cast the bodies overboard. Finally he lost consciousness and knew not whether his three remaining companions were dead or alive.

"Then he said he seemed in a dream to see a ship and tried to go to her for help, but just as he would be going on board of her something would seem to keep him back; three times in his dreams he tried to visit this ship, and the last time there seemed to come to him a certain satisfaction, and he felt that he had succeeded in his object. Turning to my table, he said: 'Let me take your chart; I'll show you just where we were.'

"'Stop,' said I, 'don't take that chart, it is an old one and all marked over. Mark your position on this new one.' He took my pencil and knife, and carefully sharpened his pencil. Then, taking my dividers, he measured his latitude and longitude and placed a pencil dot at a point on the clean chart. As he lifted his hand he said: 'Oh, excuse me, captain, I cut my finger in sharpening the pencil and have left a drop of blood on the chart.'

"'Never mind,' said I, 'leave it there.' And then I produced the old chart and there, in an exactly corresponding place was the drop of blood left by my ghostly visitor."

Then looking steadily into my face the mate solemnly added: "I can't explain this, sir, perhaps you can; but I can tell you on my honor it is God's own truth that I have told you."

THE GHOST OF WASHINGTON.

It was early on Christmas morning when John Reilly wheeled away from a picturesque little village where he had passed the previous night, to continue his cycling tour through eastern Pennsylvania. To-day his intention was to stop at Valley Forge, and then to ride on up the Schuylkill Valley, visiting in turn the many points of historical interest that lay along his route. Valley Forge, his road map indicated, was but a short distance further on. All around him were the hills and fields and roads over which Washington and his half-starved army had foraged and roamed throughout the trying winter of 1777-8—one hundred and twenty-six years ago.

It was a beautiful Christmas day, truly, and, as he wheeled along, young Reilly's thoughts were almost equally divided between the surrounding pleasant scenery and the folks at home, who, he knew very well, were assembling at just about the present time around a heavily laden Christmas tree in the front parlor. The sun rose higher and higher and Reilly pedaled on down the valley, passing every now and then quaint, pleasant-looking farmhouses, many of which, no doubt, had been built anterior to the period which had given the vicinity its history.

Arriving, finally, at a place where the road forked off in two directions, Reilly was puzzled which way to go on. There happened to be a dwelling close by. Accordingly he dismounted, left his wheel leaning against a gate-post at the side of the road, and walked up a wretchedly flagged walk leading to the house, with the idea of getting instructions from its inmates.

Situated in the center of an unkempt field of rank grass and weeds, the building lay back from the highway probably one hundred and fifty feet. It was long and low in shape, containing but one story and having what is termed a gabled roof, under which there must have been an attic of no mean size. On coming close to the house, a fact Reilly had not noticed from the road became plainly evident. It was deserted. He saw that the roof and side shingles were in wretched condition; that the window sashes and frames as well as the doors and door frames were missing from the openings in the side walls where once they had been, and that the entire side of the house, including that part of the stone foundation which showed above the ground, was full of cracks and seams. At first on the point of turning back, he concluded to see what the interior was like anyway.

Accordingly he went inside. Glancing around the large dust-filled room he had entered his gaze at first failed to locate any object of the least interest. A rickety appearing set of steps went up into the attic from one side of the apartment and over in one corner was a large open fireplace, from the walls of which much of the brickwork had become loosened and fallen out. Reilly had started up the steps toward the attic, when happening to look back for an instant, his attention was attracted to a singular-looking, jug-shaped bottle no larger than a vinegar cruet, which lay upon its side on the hearth of the fireplace, partly covered up by debris of loose bricks and mortar. He hastened back down the steps and crossed the room, taking the bottle up in his hand and examining it with curiosity. Being partly filled with a liquid of some kind or other the bottle was very soon uncorked and held under the young man's nose. The liquid gave forth a peculiar, pungent and inviting odor. Without further hesitation Reilly's lips sought the neck of the bottle. It is hardly possible to describe the pleasure and satisfaction his senses experienced as he drank.

While the fluid was still gurgling down his throat a heavy hand was placed most suddenly on his shoulder and his body was given a violent shaking. The bottle fell to the floor and was broken into a hundred pieces.

"Hello!" said a rough voice almost in Reilly's ear. "Who are you, anyway? And what are you doing within the lines? A spy, I'll be bound."

As most assuredly there had been no one else in the vicinity of the building when he had entered it and with equal certainty no one had come down the steps from the attic, Reilly was naturally surprised and mystified by this unexpected assault. He struggled instinctively to break loose from the unfriendly grasp, and when he finally succeeded he twisted his body around so that he faced across the room. Immediately he made the remarkable discovery that there were four other persons in the apartment—three uncouth-looking fellows habited in fantastic but ragged garments, and a matronly-looking woman, the latter standing over a washtub which had been elevated upon two chairs in a corner near the fireplace. To all appearance the woman had been busy at her work and had stopped for the moment to see what the men were going to do; her waist sleeves were rolled up to the shoulders and her arms dripped with water and soapsuds. Over the tops of the tubs, partly filled with water, there were visible the edges of several well-soaked fabrics. Too add to his astonishment he noticed that in the chimney-place, which a moment before was falling apart, but now seemed to be clean and in good condition, a cheerful fire burned, and that above the flames was suspended an iron pot, from which issued a jet of steam. He noticed also that the entire appearance of the room had undergone a great change. Everything seemed to be in good repair, tidy and neat; the ceilings, the walls and the door; even the stairway leading to the attic. The openings in the walls were fitted with window sashes and well-painted doors. The apartment had, in fact, evolved under his very eyesight from a state of absolute ruin into one of excellent preservation.

All of this seemed so weird and uncanny, that Reilly stood for a moment or two in the transformed apartment, utterly dumbfounded, with his mouth wide open and his eyes all but popping out of his head. He was brought to his senses by the fellow who had shaken him growling out:

"Come! Explain yourself!"

"An explanation is due me," Reilly managed to gasp.

"Don't bandy words with the rascal, Harry," one of the other men spoke up. "Bring him along to headquarters."

Thereupon, without further parley, the three men marched Reilly in military fashion into the open air and down to the road. Here he picked up at the gate-post his bicycle, while they unstacked a group of three old-fashioned-looking muskets located close by. When the young man had entered the house a few minutes before, this stack of arms had not been there. He could not understand it. Neither could he understand, on looking back at the building as he was marched off down the road, the mysterious agency that had transformed its dilapidated exterior, just as had been the interior, into a practically new condition.

While they trudged along, the strangers exhibited a singular interest in the wheel Reilly pushed at his side, running their coarse hands over the frame and handle-bar, and acting on the whole as though they never before had seen a bicycle. This in itself was another surprise. He had hardly supposed there were three men in the country so totally unacquainted with what is a most familiar piece of mechanism everywhere.

At the same time that they were paying so much attention to the wheel, Reilly in turn was studying with great curiosity his singular-looking captors. Rough, unprepossessing appearing fellows they were, large of frame and unshaven, and, it must be added, dirty of face. What remained of their very ragged clothing, he had already noticed, was of a most remarkable cut and design, resembling closely the garments worn by the Continental militiamen in the War of Independence. The hats were broad, low of crown, and three-cornered in shape; the trousers were buff-colored and ended at the knees, and the long, blue spike-tailed coats were flapped over at the extremities of the tails, the flaps being fastened down with good-sized brass buttons. Leather leggings were strapped around cowhide boots, through the badly worn feet of which, in places where the leather had cracked open, the flesh, unprotected by stockings, could be seen. Dressed as he was, in a cleanly, gray cycling costume, Reilly's appearance, most assuredly, was strongly in contrast to that of his companions.

After a brisk walk of twenty minutes, during which they occasionally met and passed by one or two or perhaps a group of men clothed and outfitted like

Reilly's escorts, the little party followed the road up a slight incline and around a well-wooded bend to the left, coming quite suddenly, and to the captive, very unexpectedly, to what was without doubt a military encampment; a village, in fact, composed of many rows of small log huts. Along the streets, between the buildings, muskets were stacked in hundreds of places. Over in one corner, on a slight eminence commanding the road up which they had come, and cleverly hidden from it behind trees and shrubbery, the young man noticed a battery of field pieces. Wherever the eye was turned on this singular scene were countless numbers of soldiers all garmented in three-cornered hats, spike-tailed coats and knee breeches, walking lazily hither and thither, grouped around crackling fires, or parading up and down the streets in platoons under the guidance of ragged but stern-looking officers.

Harry stopped the little procession of four in front of one of the larger of the log houses. Then, while they stood there, the long blast from a bugle was heard, followed by the roll of drums. A minute or two afterward, several companies of militia marched up and grounded their arms, forming three sides of a hollow square around them, the fourth and open side being toward the log house. Directly succeeding this maneuver there came through the doorway of the house and stepped up the center of the square, stopping directly in front of Reilly, a dignified-looking person, tall and straight and splendidly proportioned of figure, and having a face of great nobility and character.

The cold chills chased one another down Reilly's back. His limbs swayed and tottered beneath his weight. He had never experienced another such sensation of mingled astonishment and fright.

He was in the presence of General Washington. Not a phantom Washington, either, but Washington in the flesh and blood; as material and earthly a being as ever crossed a person's line of vision. Reilly, in his time, had seen so many portraits, marble busts and statues of the great commander that he could not be mistaken. Recovering the use of his faculties, which for the moment he seemed to have lost, Reilly did the very commonplace thing that others before him have done when placed unexpectedly in remarkable situations. He pinched himself to make sure that he was in reality wide awake and in the natural possession of his senses. He felt like pinching the figure in front of him also, but he could not muster up the courage to do that. He stood there trying to think it all out, and as his thoughts became less stagnant, his fright dissolved under the process of reasoning his mind pursued. To reason a thing out, even though an explanation can only be obtained by leaving much of the subject unaccounted for, tends to make one bolder and less shaky in the knees.

The series of strange incidents which he was experiencing had been inaugurated in the old-fashioned dwelling he had visited after information concerning the roads. And everything had been going along in a perfectly normal way up to, the very moment when he had taken a drink from the bottle found in the fireplace. But from that precise time everything had gone wrongly. Hence the inference that the drinking of the peculiar liquid was accountable in some way or other for his troubles. There was a supernatural agency in the whole thing. That much must be admitted. And whatever that agency was, and however it might be accounted for, it had taken Reilly back into a period of time more than a hundred years ago, and landed him, body and soul, within the lines of the patriot forces wintering at Valley Forge. He might have stood there, turning over and over in his mind, pinching himself and muttering, all the morning, had not the newcomer ceased a silent but curious inspection of his person, and asked: "Who are you, sir?"

"John Reilly, at your pleasure," the young man replied, adding a question on his own account: "And who are you, sir?"

Immediately he received a heavy thump on his back from Harry's hard fist.

"It is not for you to question the general," the ragged administrator of the blow exclaimed.

"And it is not for you to be so gay," Reilly returned, angrily, giving the blow back with added force.

"Here, here!" broke in the first questioner. "Fisticuffs under my very nose! No more of this, I command you both." To Harry he added an extra caution: "Your zeal in my behalf will be better appreciated by being less demonstrative. Blows should be struck only on the battlefield." To Reilly he said, with a slight smile hovering over his face, "My name is Washington. Perhaps you may have heard of me?"

To this Reilly replied: "I have, indeed, and heard you very well spoken of, too." Emboldened by the other's smile, he ventured another question: "I think my reckoning of the day and year is badly at fault. An hour ago I thought the day was Christmas day. How far out of the way did my calculation take me, sir?"

"The day is indeed Christmas day, and the year is, as you must know, the year of our Lord one thousand seven hundred and seventy-seven."

Reilly again pinched himself.

"Why do you bring this man to me?" Washington now inquired, turning to Harry and his companions.

"He is a spy, sir," said Harry.

"That is a lie!" Reilly indignantly interpolated. "I have done nothing to warrant any such charge."

"We found him in the Widow Robin's house, pouring strong liquor down his throat."

"I had gone inside after information concerning the roads——"

"Which he was getting from a bottle, sir."

"If drinking from a bottle of necessity constitutes being a spy, I fear our camp is already a hotbed," Washington somewhat sagely remarked, casting his eye around slyly at his officers and men. "Tell me," he went on, with sudden sternness, looking Reilly through and through, as though to read his very thoughts, "is the charge true? Do you come from Howe?"

"The charge is not true, sir. I come from no one. I simply am making a tour of pleasure through this part of the country on my bicycle."

"With the country swarming with the men from two hostile armies, any kind of a tour, save one of absolute necessity, seems ill-timed."

"When I set out I knew nothing about any armies. The fact is, sir——" Reilly started to make an explanation, but he checked himself on realizing that the telling of any such improbable yarn would only increase the hazardousness of his position.

"Well?" Washington questioned, in a tone of growing suspicion.

"I certainly did not know that your army or any other army was quartered in this vicinity." Reilly hesitated for lack of something further to say. "You see," he finally added, prompted by a happy idea, "I rode my wheel from New York."

"You may have come from New York, though it is hard to believe you came on that singular-looking machine so great a distance. Where is the horse which drew the vehicle?"

Reilly touched his bicycle. "This is the horse, sir, just as it is; the vehicle," he said.

"The man is crazy!" Harry exclaimed. Washington only looked the incredulity he felt, and this time asked a double question.

"How can the thing be balanced without it be held upright by a pair of shafts from a horse's back, and how is the motive power acquired?"

For an answer Reilly jumped upon the wheel, and at a considerable speed and in a haphazard way pedaled around the space within the hollow square of soldiers. Hither and thither he went, at one second nearly wheeling over the toes of the line of astonished, if not frightened, militiamen; at the next, bearing suddenly down on Harry and his companions and making them dance and jump about most alertly to avoid a collision. Even the dignified Washington was once or twice put to the necessity of dodging hurriedly aside when his equilibrium was threatened. Reilly eventually dismounted, doing so with assumed clumsiness by stopping the wheel at Harry's back and falling over heavily against the soldier. Harry tumbled to the ground, but Reilly dexterously landed on his feet. At once he began offering a profusion of apologies.

"You did that by design!" Harry shouted, jumping to his feet. His face was red with anger and he shook his fist threateningly at the bicyclist.

Washington commanded the man to hold his peace. Then to Reilly he expressed a great surprise at his performance and a desire to know more about the bicycle. The young man thereupon described the machine minutely, lifting it into the air and spinning the wheels to illustrate how smoothly they rotated.

"I can see it is possible to ride the contrivance with rapidity. It has been put together with wonderful ingenuity," Washington said, when Reilly had replaced the wheel on the ground.

"And you, sir, it is but a toy," an officer spoke up. "Put our friend on his bundle of tin and race him against one of our horsemen and he would make a sorry showing."

Reilly smiled. "I bear the gentleman no ill-will for his opinion," he said. "Still, I should like to show him by a practical test of the subject that his ignorance of it is most profound."

"You would test the speed of the machine against that of a horse?" Washington said, in amazement.

"I would, sir. You have a good road yonder. With your permission and a worthy opponent I would make the test at once."

"But, sir, the man is a spy," Harry broke in. "Would it not be better to throw a rope around his neck and give him his deserts?"

"The charge is by no means proven," Washington replied. "Nor can it be until a court martial convenes this afternoon. And I see no reason why we may not in the meantime enjoy the unique contest which has been suggested. It will make a pleasant break in the routine of camp life."

A murmur of approval went up from the masses of men by whom they were surrounded. While they had been talking it seemed as though everybody in the camp not already on the scene had gathered together behind the square of infantry.

"Then, sir," Harry said, with some eagerness, "I would like to be the man to ride the horse. There is no better animal than mine anywhere. And I understand his tricks and humors quite well enough to put him to his best pace."

"I confess I have heard you well spoken of as a horseman," Washington said. "Be away with you! Saddle and bridle your horse at once."

It was the chain of singular circumstances narrated above which brought John Reilly into the most remarkable contest of his life. He had entered many bicycle races at one time or other, always with credit to himself and to the club whose colors he wore. And he had every expectation of making a good showing to-day. Yet a reflection of the weird conditions which had brought about the present contest took away some of his self-possession when a few minutes later he was marched over to the turnpike and left to his own thoughts, while the officers were pacing out a one mile straightaway course down the road.

After the measurements had been taken, two unbroken lines of soldiers were formed along the entire mile; a most evident precaution against Reilly leaving the race course at any point to escape across the fields. Washington came up to him again, when the preparations were completed, to shake his hand and whisper a word or two of encouragement in his ear. Having performed these kindly acts he left to take up a position near the point of finish.

The beginning of the course was located close to the battery of half concealed field pieces. Reilly was now conducted to this place. Shortly afterward Harry appeared on his horse. He leered at the bicyclist contemptuously and said something of a sarcastic nature partly under his breath when the two lined up, side by side, for the start. To these slights Reilly paid no heed; he had a strong belief that when the race was over there would be left in the mutton-like head of his opponent very little of his present inclination toward the humorous. The soldier's mount was a handsome black mare, fourteen and a half hands high; strong of limbs and at the flanks, and animated by a spirit that kept her prancing around with continuous action. It must be admitted that the man rode very well. He guided the animal with ease and nonchalance when she reared and plunged, and kept her movements confined to an incredibly small piece of ground, considering her abundance of action.

"Keep to your own side of the road throughout the race. I don't want to be collided with by your big beast," Reilly cautioned, while they were awaiting two signals from the starter.

To this Harry replied in some derision, "I'll give you a good share of the road at the start, and all of it and my dust, too, afterward." And then the officer who held the pistol fired the first shot.

Reilly was well satisfied with the conditions under which the race was to be made. The road was wide and level, smooth, hard and straight, and a strong breeze which had sprung up, blew squarely against his back. His wheel was geared up to eighty-four inches; the breeze promised to be a valuable adjunct in pushing it along. Awaiting the second and last signal, Reilly glanced down the two blue ranks of soldiers, which stretched away into hazy lines in the distance and converged at the termination of the course where a flag had been stuck into the ground. The soldiers were at parade rest. Their unceasing movements as they chatted to one another, turning their bodies this way and that and craning their heads forward to look toward the starting point, and then jerking them back, made the lines seem like long, squirming snakes. At the end of the course a thick bunch of militiamen clogged the road and overspread into the fields.

Crack! The signal to be off. Reilly shoved aside the fellow who had been holding his wheel upright while astride of it, and pushed down on the pedals. The mare's hoofs dug the earth; her great muscular legs straightened out; she sprang forward with a snort of apparent pleasure, taking the lead at the very start. Reilly heard the shout of excitement run along the two ranks of soldiers. He saw them waving their arms and hats as he went by. And on ahead through the cloud of dust there was visible the shadow-like outlines of the snorting, galloping horse, whose hoof beats sounded clear and sharp above the din which came from the sides of the highway. The mare crept farther and farther ahead. Very soon a hundred feet or more of the road lay between her and the bicyclist. Harry turned in his saddle and called out another sarcasm.

"I shall pass you very soon. Keep to your own side of the road!" Reilly shouted, not a bit daunted by the way the race had commenced. His head was well down over the handle-bars, his back had the shape of the upper portion of an immense egg. Up and down his legs moved; faster and faster and faster yet. He went by the soldiers so rapidly that they only appeared to be two streaks of blurry color. Their sharp rasping shouts sounded like the cracking of musketry. The cloud of dust blew against the bicyclist's head and into his mouth and throat. When he glanced ahead again he saw with satisfaction that the mare was no longer increasing her lead. It soon became evident even that he was slowly cutting down the advantages she had secured.

Harry again turned his head shortly afterward, doubtless expecting to find his opponent hopelessly distanced by this time. Instead of this Reilly was alarmingly close upon him. The man ejaculated a sudden oath and lashed his animal furiously. Straining every nerve and sinew the mare for the moment pushed further ahead. Then her pace slackened a bit and Reilly again crept up to her. Closer and closer to her than before, until his head was abreast of her outstretched tail. Harry was lashing the mare and swearing at her unceasingly now. But she had spurted once and appeared to be incapable of again increasing her speed. In this way they went on for some little distance, Harry using his whip brutally, the mare desperately struggling to attain a greater pace, Reilly hanging on with tenacity to her hind flanks and giving up not an inch of ground.

A mile is indeed a very short distance when traversed at such a pace. The finishing flag was already but a few hundred feet further on. Reilly realized that it was time now to go to the front. He gritted his teeth together with determination and bent his head down even further toward his front wheel. Then his feet began to move so quickly that there was only visible an indistinct blur at the sides of his crank shaft. At this very second, with a face marked with rage and hatred, Harry brought his horse suddenly across the road to thet part of it which he had been warned to avoid.

It is hard to tell what kept Reilly from being run into and trampled under foot. An attempt at back pedaling, a sudden twist of the handle-bar, a lurch to one side that almost threw him from his seat. Then, in the fraction of a second he was over on the other side of the road, pushing ahead of the mare almost as though she were standing still. The outburst of alarm from the throats of the soldiers changed when they saw that Reilly had not been injured; first into a shout of indignation at the dastardly attempt which had been made to run him down, and then into a roar of delight when the bicyclist breasted the flag a winner of the race by twenty feet.

As he crossed the line Reilly caught a glimpse of Washington. He stood close to the flag and was waving his hat in the air with the enthusiasm of a schoolboy. Reilly went on down the road slackening his speed as effectively as he could. But before it was possible to entirely stop his wheel's momentum the noisy acclamations in his rear ceased with startling suddenness. He turned in his saddle and looked back. As sure as St. Peter he had the road entirely to himself. There wasn't a soldier or the ghost of a soldier in sight.

As soon as he could he turned his bicycle about and rode slowly back along the highway, now so singularly deserted, looking hither and thither in vain for some trace of the vanished army. Even the flag which had been stuck into the ground at the end of the one-mile race course was gone. The breeze had died out again and the air was tranquil and warm. In the branches of a nearby tree two sparrows chirped and twittered peacefully. Reilly went back to the place where the camp had been. He found there only open fields on one side of the road and a clump of woodland on the other. He continued on down the little hill up which Harry and his companions had brought him a few hours previously and followed the road on further, coming finally to the fork in it near which was located the old farmhouse wherein he had been taken captive. The house was, as it had been when he had previously entered it, falling apart from age and neglect. When he went inside he found lying on the brick hearth in front of the fireplace a number of pieces of broken glass.

THE END.

Milton Keynes UK
Ingram Content Group UK Ltd.
UKHW030908151124
451262UK00006B/907

9 789362 519771